RED HILL

To Sherry,
Hope you enjoy the
book.
Thank you very much!

RED HILL

BENSON JACKSON

Blue
Door
PUBLISHING

CHAPTER 1

OCTOBER 25

The sun had just come up over the trees on a calm fall morning in Red Hill, Indiana. As Bob gazed out his kitchen window, he frowned. The pumpkins had all been harvested from the neighboring fields. 2016 was almost over. There was a light amount of frost that reminded everyone that winter was on its way to the Midwest.

After getting his morning coffee ready to go, Bob Felzer made his way outside and started warming up his Ford Bronco for the drive to work. The Bronco was ancient but reliable. Bob debated getting a new paint job on the old girl after Christmas with the yearly safety bonus he would receive. He thought a red and white color scheme would be a good replacement for Ford blue. On the other hand, if one of his kids wanted to go back to school, he might use the bonus for tuition.

RED HILL

As Bob approached the interstate, his favorite radio program, *The Bob and Tom Show*, began. On the show's agenda today was prerecorded guest Haywood Banks singing his song "Orange Barrels." Bob chuckled to himself as orange barrel season was almost over in Indiana. Most of the road construction ended about mid-October.

Bob's house was on the northern side of Red Hill, which was a town of about twenty thousand but with a smaller, hometown feel. During the drive to work, Bob reminisced about the many years he had traveled the world in the navy and lived in many places in the United States and abroad, but Red Hill had called to him when he retired. His children were still there.

How much time did I miss with my children when I was in the navy? Will I ever really connect to them in ways that other fathers do? My children are now adults, but they're also slackers who need direction.

Work intruded on his thoughts, as he scanned the AM channels for the weather station. It was only a few weeks till vacation, but work was stressful with some of the personalities he managed.

Why am I scanning AM? There are far more channels on the FM band.

Bob pressed the FM button when something sprung up in his peripheral vision. *Damn!* Mashing the brakes and twisting the wheel, he created a fishtail effect in the path of the Bronco. The tumbler full of coffee bounced around the passenger seat and landed on the passenger-side floorboard. A whitetail deer ran halfway across the road and then turned back. In his rearview mirror, the deer then darted back across the road following its original path. Memories of the one he hit before on this road returned. It had been a few years ago, but the repair bill had been enough to make Bob install a brush guard on his truck. He had completed the mechanical repairs himself before taking it to the body shop. *Should I buy a third Bronco for parts?* He and his son had already purchased two. They enjoyed restoring them together. It had been one of the few things that the father and son enjoyed doing together as his children reached adulthood.

Is the chill I feel the weather or the adrenaline rush?

He was ready for a hopefully uneventful day at work. Bob's employer for the last nine years had been the Red Hill Nuclear Power Plant. The dreaded shift turnover between one of his newer employees, Raymond Church, and a night-shift employee, Earl Finn, would happen this morning. Those two were continually fighting over miniscule details, sometimes at a level that might eventually have to be dealt with by human resources or maybe even security. Bob didn't want to deal with this today. But if he had to, at least he was now awake. In the navy, dealing with this situation would have been much easier. Civilian life suited Bob, but he missed some of the order in his former job.

The rest of the drive was not as exciting. He changed the radio station to the country station and did something he hadn't done since the 1980s: he reached into his shirt pocket for a cigarette. He hadn't purchased a pack since Oliver North had taken the stand in the Iran Contra Affair. *Why am I reaching for my smokes?* He put this out of his mind as he displayed his badge for the security guard and scanner that allowed him to enter the parking lot. Ahead of him in the line was Raymond Church's

Subaru. Maybe he could speak to him about his arguments with Earl Finn before they walked into work.

After parking beside Raymond and getting his lunch box, they walked to the turnstile together where they would once again display their badges to enter the site.

As they walked, Bob spoke. "Raymond, I know you and Earl don't see eye to eye on a lot of stuff, but you've got to turn down the heat on this. He's old and has a very short temper. I also believe he's retiring in another couple of months. So be patient and don't let him get to you. You don't want any sort of write-up in your file. It takes six months for those to go off your record. There's going to be at least one supervisor spot opening soon, and you'll be a good candidate if your HR file's clear." Bob felt fatherly as he dispensed this advice.

"I understand, but Earl is starting to slide—not just a little, but a lot. His mistakes could put the plant and the community in danger," Raymond replied.

Bob considered this against the fail-safes in the plant. "Trust me, he's getting a write-up for his lack of attention to detail. Maybe it'll piss him off enough for him to hang it up."

"I won't miss his red face and pink shirt and dog-shit breath when he goes," Raymond quipped.

Bob grinned as he replied, "I don't know anyone who will."

Bob entered the control room with his code. Raymond followed after entering his code. The control room was the brains of the nuclear power plant, where all equipment was remotely monitored and operated. The lights were kept dim so that operators would be able to see the screens in detail. Even minor variances in equipment status were recorded, reported, and scrutinized.

Bob started his shift turnover with Howard Wurtz, occasionally glancing over at the turnover that was happening between Raymond and Earl.

After covering reading sheets, standing orders, and procedural changes, Howard mentioned one oddity. "For some reason around 2 a.m., camera NE-E 24 started to malfunction. It started to move and change focus without being operated by any of our operators. We sent an I&C tech out to look at it, and he couldn't find anything wrong. Continue to monitor it today," Howard said.

"That's definitely odd. I'll make sure that one of our people checks it at least hourly today," Bob replied.

Howard knew as well as Bob that electrical and mechanical components do not move themselves. The most reasonable explanation for this would have been a prank by some bored operator. A much more sinister possibility would be industrial sabotage by a very talented hacker.

CHAPTER 2

Hanna Green's alarm clock went off at 6:55 a.m. Normally, she dreaded waking up this early, but today was different. This was Friday, and she had it planned in detail. She was going to work a half-day and then catch a movie with Cindy Peller, one of her old friends from college. The years since graduation were going by faster than she liked. The passage of time reminded her of some saying that she had heard her mother say: *The only way that time grows is shorter.*

Hanna had taken a job as the business manager for a check-into-cash place after marrying a man named Gary who worked at the power plant. The first five and a half years of their marriage had been great. The last year of their union had been very difficult.

Gary had come home after work on a rainy afternoon and sat in his recliner. He was flipping through the channels and pretended that he didn't even notice the tow truck that stopped in front of their house and started to repossess her Honda.

RED HILL

When Hanna asked Gary what was happening, he calmly explained that he had been gambling on boxing matches. He had blown through their savings, Taylor's college fund, and now the title to her car. This lack of savings made getting the divorce difficult, but absolute.

This had happened over two years ago, and Hanna was indifferent to Red Hill. She had moved here with Gary. She often considered moving to a larger city such as Indianapolis or Chicago. Red Hill was a very safe town, but opportunities were far and few between. She was not thinking of this now. She was now thinking about the difficulty of dragging her son Taylor out of bed. She found it funny that on Christmas morning and on his birthday, he would have already been up and ready to start the day's festivities. But on a random Friday, with nothing but the promise of second-grade schoolwork, he was a very late riser.

She grabbed a quick shower and started working on her hair.

CHAPTER 3

OCTOBER 26

Roper Thompson's head hurt, and he was getting the chills that always happened when he ran out of drugs. He had been a frequent meth user until the last few months when heroin started showing up in his small social circle. Roper's childhood had been unremarkable. He had been a Cub Scout, as his father had, and a member of 4H with his sister. Both of their parents had high hopes for their children, which fizzled and died in their teenage years.

Roper and Ashley had always been close. When Ashley had started to experiment with drugs, so did Roper. Shortly before Ashley's seventeenth birthday, she overdosed and died. This had sent Roper into a drug-fueled depression from which he would never escape.

His grandparents had used much of their retirement money to help Roper get clean. He sometimes wanted a sober life, doing some of the things he saw people do on TV such as hanging out in a coffee shop, maybe with a beautiful young woman, or joining the military, like his uncle Roy. But these thoughts often came between binges.

He also knew that his criminal record would keep him out of the military or from being able to get a good job in a town with a nice coffeehouse. Sometimes the local sheriff, Tim Baylor, would arrest him. Roper had considered killing the sheriff several times when he was using, but luckily, he had never run into him when he felt like this. He knew that he would live and die in Red Hill, probably spending much of that time in jail.

Roper's grandfather had left him a small farm and a house. Roper had lost both of those with his drug habits. He didn't mind. He didn't want to be a farmer, or anything else. He just wanted to get high again soon. His usual hustle was stealing whatever he could find of value and pawning it in the next town over. This would often be enough for a small fix, and sometimes a night's stay at the Happy Hoosier Motel.

He was standing in the parking lot of the motel now. An old man in a powder-blue Chevrolet S-10 with a Domino's sign pulled into the parking lot. The old man set the manual transmission to neutral, set the parking brake, and hopped out in one smooth motion. What he did not do, however, was lock the door.

Cindy Peller was getting ready for bed. She had spent six hours on the road after leaving work. Cindy had considered driving all the way to Hanna's house on this evening, but instead, she decided to stop at the Happy Hoosier Motel. The Happy Hoosier seemed like an ugly little sister of the Motel 6. The room had a slight odor to it, and the heater looked a little sketchy. The remote for the TV had a cable that attached to the nightstand. She grinned as a scenario flashed through her mind about an imaginary newspaper article that read, "International Remote Thieves Foiled by Happy Hoosier Antitheft Cable." The grin became an out-loud laugh when she opened the bathroom to see that the plunger was not only present in the bathroom, but also cabled to a bracket on the wall.

After making sure that the bed was relatively comfy, she decided the motel would do, just for one night. Although this place was named the Happy Hoosier and there was a four-foot print of Larry Bird above the front desk, she still couldn't get over how much this place reminded her of a Motel 6.

She had stayed at a Motel 6 once in high school. Her mother had driven her three hours away to see Stone Temple Pilots her freshman year. The concert had ended late, and Motel 6 was the first place they had found to stay on the way back. This room looked almost the same as the one she could remember from the early 1990s.

She was looking through her phone for some '90s music when someone knocked on her door. There was not a peephole in the door, and without asking who was there, against her better judgement, she opened the door.

"Pizza pizza," an old man in a Domino's hat said.

"Isn't that the Little Caesar's slogan?" Cindy asked.

"I suppose, but I doubt they mind." The old man returned the smile and started to look at the order ticket.

"I didn't order a pizza," Cindy replied.

"I did." A nervous-looking young Asian man approached Cindy and the old man standing in the doorway of Room 109.

"The ticket says Room 109, but it could have been a mistake," the old man said.

"Could it have been Room 105?" asked the nervous-looking young man.

"Pepperoni and green olive?" asked the delivery man.

"Yes, thank you," replied the man, looking over his shoulder.

The young nervous man handed a twenty to the old man, grabbed his pizza, and returned to Room 105 without saying another word. Cindy thought that the young man acted very odd, as though he did not want to be seen or noticed, but she let the thought go as she was still standing there in silence with the delivery man.

"He must be here for the Bridge Festival; it brings out all kinds," the old man said.

"Must be. Have a good night," replied Cindy.

As Cindy shut the door, she remembered the bridge festival. Its real name was the Covered Bridge Festival, and it brought in a lot of revenue to the local area, but it had been over for weeks. *Why did the young guy buying the pizza seem so nervous? Why do I care?* She decided that she didn't. It was time for bed.

The old man who delivered the pizza was named Roger Smith. Roger was also dismissing the strange-acting young man to whom he had delivered the pizza as he found another man going through his truck.

"What the hell are you doing?" Roger asked the man, although from the looks of the clothing on the man, he thought he knew the answer without having to be told.

Roper had been looking in the glove box for money. He found none. The old man startled him.

Roger looked over the desperate man who had been rummaging through his truck. The man was at least forty years younger than him. Roger started to regret yelling at him.

Roper looked at the old man. If Roper would have had his fix, he could have easily fought the old man. But he was weak, and getting weaker. He staggered away into the darkness.

Roger considered calling the police, but after a quick look through his vehicle, he determined that nothing had been taken. He placed his key in the ignition. He would be locking his truck from now on.

CHAPTER 4

OCTOBER 27

Janice Harmon was making sandwiches. Her favorite was pimento cheese. Her neighbor Frank Coleman seemed to like them too. She was eighty-eight years old and every bit as spry and spirited as she was at seventy-eight. Even though she could get her mail or her paper, she didn't mind when Frank brought it over in the morning.

Frank had retired from the fire department a few months ago, and this was the highlight of her day. She was way too old for romance, especially with a man that much younger than her, but before he started coming over, she rarely interacted with anyone unless she went to buy groceries. If her sons came over, which had become more and more of a rare occurrence, they might notice the small dent in the side of her car and try to stop her from even driving to the store. That would be the end of her independence, so she rarely complained that they didn't visit.

Her husband, William Harmon, had passed away over fifteen years ago, and many of her friends had passed away, which made any addition to her social circle a welcome addition. Frank was an easy person to talk to and a good listener. In the years since she had retired from teaching, she often missed having people listen to the things that she had to say. He was also handy around the house. He had fixed the kitchen drain last week and volunteered to clean out the gutters on her house later this week, which was something that her sons were not likely to do.

Today was just like many that had passed before. Frank came in with the paper and sat down at what she had deemed his end of the table. There was sun tea in the window. But it was a little too early for that.

The coffee was almost brewed. Most days, he skipped right to the ad section to see what the new gun store was advertising. Shootem was the name that was coming to her, but she knew that wasn't right. But today, he was reading the front page. Front page in the local paper usually didn't mean anything here. It was usually news from a larger town that left Red Hill sleepily unaffected.

The elections were happening soon, and this bothered her. The current governor seemed like a genuine, nice man, who really cared about the state. His name was Irwin Poole, and he was doing his best to bring jobs to this state. His opponent seemed very insincere and shallow, probably the type who was just after the job for the power.

Janice had voted a straight Republican ticket for as many elections as she could remember, and last time they had done well, but the Republicans of today weren't the Republicans of yesteryear; that was for certain. *But they might keep us from going bankrupt,* she hoped.

Janice had listened to her sons lecture her repeatedly about the pitfalls of voting a straight party ticket, but she could not see what the Democrats were doing to earn her vote. She let her mind drift for only a few seconds longer before turning her attention back to Frank. What was he reading so intently?

"What is it?" Janice asked.

"Oh, just an article written about some new state funding. They've decided to add extra funds for training local fire departments in response to incidents at nuclear power plants," he responded.

The nuclear power plant on the outskirts of town had always worried Janice. She remembered Chernobyl like it was yesterday. She was still teaching elementary school in 1986. The children of the employees at the Red Hill Nuclear Power Plant asked her if the same thing could happen here. She had told them American reactors were built much better than the Soviet ones. She knew very little about nuclear power, but in the patriotic 1980s, the children seemed happy with the explanation. A few years back, there had been a meltdown in Japan caused by a tsunami. She remembered being relieved at the time that she didn't have to explain that one to young children.

"Should we be worried about the one here?" asked Janice.

"Nah, we used to get training in these sorts of things all the time. It's just odd to me since there are so many things that my guys could have used the funding for. Nuclear incidents are bad, but we haven't had one in the United States since Three Mile Island. That was a long time ago. The funding here should go to another tanker truck," replied Frank.

CHAPTER 5

OCTOBER 28

Taylor Green had a wonderful day. His mom had taken him for pizza and ice cream on a weeknight, which she had only started doing recently. After this, it was off to the drugstore to buy this year's Halloween costume.

There was only one thing that he wanted to be for Halloween: a Bash'em Badger. There were six of them in the cartoon based on the book series, but his favorite was Pol (pronounced Paul).

In the first book about the adventures and how the badgers got started, it was determined that Pol got his name and powers from some sort of nuclear reactor. Pol was short for polonium 210, which his mother had said was awful. Of course, that probably meant that whatever it was, was in fact cool. Pol also had the red karate belt. Red was Taylor's favorite color. The black belt was reserved for the badger named Atom, (pronounced Adam).

His mom reluctantly read him a chapter of the story before bed every night, even though she didn't like the story and didn't think that Taylor needed to hear every detail in it. He was oblivious to this and didn't realize that some of the story's content had been edited by Mom for his listening pleasure.

After coming home with the costume, it was playtime. He dressed as Pol and proceeded to protect their home from all sorts of evil. The plastic sword that came with the costume was flimsy, and his mom had warned him several times that if he broke it, he wouldn't have it on Halloween.

Throwing caution to the wind, Taylor went back to the business of ridding his house of wrongdoers. He ran laps around the kitchen island chasing imaginary foes with their golden retriever Beau, who was still up to the task of running. For how much longer, Hanna didn't know.

At 8:30 p.m., with most of the Bash'em Badger's foes being decimated, it was time for bed. He hung the sword on the headboard of his bed and pondered Halloween. Candy was imminent. He also knew that he would probably get more candy this Halloween than last. Since his dad had left, his mom had relaxed on many of her rules, and although he missed his dad, he also liked getting his way. If only this worked on his friends. He had two: TJ and Larry. TJ was happy to pretend that he was Atom, but Larry also wanted to be Pol. This had created some friction in the group, so much friction that their teacher, Mrs. Couch, had to call both of their moms last week. *Maybe if I gave Larry some of my candy, he would pick another badger to be at playtime.*

Much to Taylor's delight, when he crossed the threshold from awake to dreamland, Atom was waiting for him along with another badger named Al. Al was short for alpha wave radiation, although Taylor had no idea what that meant.

"How's it going, Pol?" Atom asked Taylor.

They were standing on top of the water tower on the outskirts of town. It was a warm, sunny day with a light breeze, and why wouldn't they be? Water towers were a favorite hangout for badger adventures.

"Awesome Possum!" Taylor exclaimed, remembering Pol's favorite catchphrase. He looked down at what had been the body of a seven-year-old in elementary school a few minutes ago to see the grown body of a warrior in the form of a badger. He swung his sword to the sky, excited to do what he believed was his life's calling. Then he asked with equal excitement what they wanted to do next.

"I want to eat!" Al said.

"Me too!" said Atom.

Taylor looked at them. "We could go out for pizza!"

"Where are we going to get pizza?" asked Atom.

Taylor looked at his badger friend. "At the Pizza Shack. I went there this afternoon with Mom. They have video games and ice cream and a machine where you can win prizes!"

"There is no more Pizza Shack. No more ice cream, and the machines are in embers," Al said with a look of anger that Taylor hadn't noticed before. He then took a step closer to Taylor and continued to talk. "Do you know how Bash'em Badgers are made?"

Taylor considered it for a second and then shrugged his shoulders.

"It takes a nuclear meltdown. A nuclear meltdown is required to make a Bash'em Badger. Look behind you," Al stated.

Taylor turned around and looked back toward the town. The town which had been sunny a minute ago was now dark with debris in the air all around him. It was getting hard to breathe, and he could see a rising cloud pushing everything he had ever known away, much like when he had used the garden hose on an anthill.

Al had been correct. There was no more Pizza Shack. There was no more anything. His house was gone. There was a cloud in the sky over where his dad worked that reached miles into the sky—black, narrow at the bottom, and then expanding as it rose.

Standing in this one spot, Taylor could see it all. His day care was burning; the drugstore where he bought his Halloween costume was also burning. The nice lady who had sold him his costume was smoking with large open eyes that seemed to be looking at him and a mouth that was now permanently open.

He turned back around in fear, only then noticing that Al and Atom had closed what little distance there had been between them.

Taylor was now sobbing. "We can do something about this! We are the Bash'em Badgers!"

"No, *we* are the Bash'em Badgers. You are a little boy. And we haven't eaten for a while," Al responded.

Taylor looked back down at his body expecting to see a fierce badger body, only to see the body of a child once again. Two full sets of razor-sharp teeth belonging to Al and Atom were closing in on him. A familiar odor, the stench of something he recognized but couldn't remember, wafted his way on the heat of their breath.

As Al's teeth tore into his cheek, he began to scream. Blood spurted out of his face as the badger's teeth tore away enough flesh to expose Taylor's teeth.

Atom was holding him down by his arm until he bit into Taylor's hand hard enough to rip it from his body. "AHHH!" was the only sound he could make as he turned and jumped off the water tower.

Taylor then remembered the smell. It was the smell of the dead cat that had been hit in front of his house in the heat of the summer.

As he fell through the air, he remembered his mom and dad arguing about cleaning it up. The argument turned into a shouting match. But this time when he went downstairs to investigate, he entered the kitchen to see that his parents' faces had been replaced by those of badgers. He screamed again and held this scream until he woke up in his bed covered in a cold sweat.

Beau was watching him during all of this and cuddled up to Taylor. Beau's fur soon soaked up most of the sweat, and after what seemed like an eternity to Taylor, he calmed down and reached over to his nightstand where his pencil box of art supplies was. He slowly took out the round-tip scissors and began to cut up the mask into unrecognizable pieces.

Hanna's hair was done, or at least as good as it was going to be done today, she thought. She was running late but could still catch up in the crucial lunch-packing stage of her morning. She wouldn't be requiring a lunch today, due to her plans, but Taylor would need something. She laughed to herself when she thought about just throwing some fruit snacks and a pudding cup in his lunch. He would probably like this, but his teacher, Mrs. Couch, probably would not.

She looked at the ridiculous food chart on the fridge. It was the same food pyramid that they had used when she was a child, only with highlighted details from each food group of the things the children were forbidden to bring, such as peanut butter.

She opened the fridge and started gathering. One healthy, hypoallergenic lunch packed, and she was starting to catch up some of the time she had lost earlier. The only obstacle in her way from leaving on time was Taylor.

Hanna turned and started walking down the hallway. Between her room and his, she was starting to see little pieces of something cut into almost confetti-sized chunks. As she studied them closer, it did look like red and white confetti.

She stooped to pick up a piece of the paper. *It's plastic.* When she had picked it up, she saw it was one of the white pieces. She turned it over to see that it was red on the other side with black lines. *Is this his Halloween mask? And if it is, why did he do this?* He had begged her to let him go this year as one of his favorited cartoon characters, whose theme song was ingrained in her head. They were the Bash'em Badgers.

She shook her head, not knowing why; there was no one awake to see it. But this was his favorite cartoon that he had to see every day, even in reruns.

Baffled at this behavior, she contemplated an interesting conversation on the way to school.

CHAPTER 6

David Harland and Shawn Graves were just finishing business for the day. Their business, 5 to 2 Doughnuts, was just starting to operate in the black. David didn't figure it would take too long. Their fiercest competition for breakfast food was David's former employer, Waffle House, and they didn't serve doughnuts.

Shawn had recently come home from the army for the last time. He had been injured in a Humvee accident a few months ago. His father heavily criticized his choice to drive a tank in the army. He had told Shawn that being a tank crewman would prepare him for exactly zero jobs when he got out of the army. Shawn had no illusions that his hometown would need a tank driver. He had just hoped to make a career of it and come back to enjoy a simple retirement.

David had just finished auto repair school at the local college, and there were no job openings for a novice mechanic within forty miles. Red Hill Auto Body hadn't hired anyone in ten years. He was considering moving to a larger town with better job prospects when they came up with the idea for the doughnut shop.

David had come up with the idea with Shawn over a few beers one night in the previous November. They had taken David's Nova out for a drive. David bought this car in high school, and he had hoped to fix it up a little with some of his earnings from his first job.

They had been driving around the town square where they had run into Shawn's uncle Paul. Paul invited them into Rusty's Pub for some beer. Paul was the odd man out in the Graves family since he had left for college at an early age and had only returned in late 2008 after his bank closed. Shawn knew that in the collapse of 2008, some banks were bailed out, and some weren't. He supposed that the bank Paul worked for was one of the ones that weren't.

They asked Paul what type of business would do well in Red Hill. After a few beers and several bad ideas later, ranging from strip club to laundromat, the three of them came up with the idea of a doughnut shop in the foreclosed gas station on the outskirts of town. It was close enough for local traffic, and it was on the way to the power plant, which should bring a lot of business.

Paul, who had helped finance several small businesses in his early banking days, helped them with their business plan and to find the best type of loan to finance the business.

CHAPTER 7

As 5 to 2 Doughnuts was starting to take off, another business about a mile away was closing. Joe Reece was trying to figure out how to keep his business alive. He owned Bull Creek Military Surplus and Gun Store. Or at least he would for a few months longer.

He pondered over his morning cup of coffee, which had recently started becoming vodka and coffee, wondering what he could do to sell more of the store's inventory. His modest selection of firearms had brought in enough locals, but when some of his other supplies hadn't sold, he'd had to raise his gun prices.

Joe had been a military man, a career soldier, until the cutbacks of the Clinton administration had forced him out early. He worked as a long-haul trucker for a few years after that. Bull Creek Military Surplus and Gun Store had been his retirement dream.

Shoot'em Up Gun and MMA Supplies had opened in Terre Haute about twenty miles away. They had deeper pockets and could afford to buy ammo in bulk and sell it cheap. They also had an indoor gun range.

If raising his prices hadn't been the straw that broke the camel's back, then Shoot'em Up was. Still, he wasn't too worried. The days of having a wife and kid to support were long over. His wife had died over twenty years ago, and the only time their daughter Tara came around anymore was on a few holidays, and those meetings were usually awkward. Tara had followed in her dad's footsteps by joining the military. He signed the papers for her to join the Air Force when she was seventeen. After four years of service, she went to school in Texas to become an accountant. She was now a CPA, and Joe couldn't be prouder.

But the years after her mom's passing had been hard on them both. Other than their shared military service, they had little to talk about. Joe often wondered if she was seeing anyone, a topic that she always changed when he asked.

The fact that he had chosen to invest more into army surplus than into guns was probably what made him more vulnerable to competition. In retrospect, he laughed. *Who buys army underwear when you can buy a four-pack of comfy underwear made in China at any department store around for half price? No one polishes their boots anymore, including the army, and no one really goes camping anymore. If they do, they take those oversize monstrosities called motor homes, complete with a bed, shower, AC, satellite, and possibly a hot tub. Not really camping,* he thought. *More like just putting a house in the woods.*

His main customers were teenagers and preteens. Young boys still marveled at how a compass worked or the functionality of a canteen cup. At least until they discovered girls. But even these customers were few and far between these days. Overworked parents often introduced them to video games at a young age and then wondered why they were so lazy later.

Joe had remembered seeing a news report that the army was worried that within ten years from now, most young people would be too fat to enlist.Disgusting. Where had he seen this? It wasn't CNN or Fox. He disliked watching either of them. In his mind, they were like two children competing to tell the biggest lie to get a piece of candy.

He poured a little more vodka into his coffee and got back to figuring out if he could save his business.

CHAPTER 8

Geonwon thought he smelled the faint odor of beer as he ordered a dozen doughnuts and a coffee. Shawn poured him a cup from 5 to 2 Doughnuts's first major purchase, which was a restaurant-grade Bunn coffee maker.

Geonwon sat at the table closest to the counter and relaxed for the first time in days. He pondered whether it would be worse to be remembered in history as a terrorist or as someone who died in a North Korean labor camp.

As a child, he had been exceptionally good at math. This may have predetermined his fate. When entering the North Korean Army at seventeen, he was immediately selected to work at a coding facility deep in the Ahobiryong Mountains.

Geonwon was among the top three coders in his class. In less than two years, he was promoted to sergeant. This would have been unheard of for most of his countrymen. Many of them worked on farms as part of their daily duty. It took many years of soldiering as an infantryman to make it to the rank of sergeant. In the cyberdivision, a soldier could advance faster if highly skilled. His family rejoiced at the news. Geonwon could send home enough money for his family to shop at the mega stores in Pyongyang. Those mega stores seemed sad after shopping at a weird supermarket called Great Scott on the drive to Red Hill.

Upon promotion, he became a level-one hacker for the government. This meant a change in duty station for Geonwon. He was not told where his new duty station would be. His newly assigned a mentor, Captain Kahn, escorted Geonwon on the train to his new duties.

The train stopped in Kimhyongjik on the border with China. Geonwon knew of the secret divisions in the People's Army across the border. He hoped that he had been picked for this duty.

Captain Kahn informed Geonwon that they would spend the night at the hotel before continuing their journey in the morning. He gave him a stern warning to go only to his hotel room, reminding him that he was not to wander about town.

Geonwon showered with nice-smelling soap under a lukewarm shower. Afterward, he hopped into bed and continued reading the novel that he had started on the train. It was about the patriotic adventures of a young DPRK couple fighting off the American army until almost their last breath. The Americans were advancing on their farming village and killing many loyal citizens of his beloved country. When only the protagonist and his wife were left to face certain doom, the Dear Leader appeared from the clouds. The Dear Leader made the skies turn dark and rain for ten days. Then, the Americans were washed out to sea.

Geonwon believed that defeating America could be done. He knew that his duties were important to that mission. But he laughed as he dismissed this story as a fairytale to read to children. He put the novel on the nightstand and turned out the light. The water dripping from the bathroom faucet kept him from sleeping. Geonwon got out of bed and twisted the knob on the shower even tighter. It still dripped.

He was walking back to the bed when the liquor cabinet called his name. The choices Geonwon normally had for alcohol were either homemade or low-quality spirits from China. This place was stocked with spirits from China, Europe, and the United States.

It would be a nice experience to try one of the bourbons from the decadent West. It would be an even nicer experience if the bourbon was terrible. No one in his family would have ever experienced Western spirts. Telling them how terrible the drinks are in the West, and how he knew, would be a fun conversation to have with his parents when he went home on leave.

The first American brand that caught his eye was Weller. He poured himself a double. It burned slightly as it went down, and it warmed his body. *Maybe one more.* This was not going to be a fun story to tell.

The room was modestly furnished except for the extravagant liquor cabinet. The bed was softer that he was used to, but comfy. The pictures of the eternal leader and his son gazed upon Geonwon in disapproval as he settled down to sleep with the rest of the Weller.

There was a knock on his door. Geonwon knew no one here other than Captain Kahn. The captain was there when he opened the door, but in front of him was a girl who couldn't have been more than sixteen.

"She is here to keep you company." The captain pushed her into the room and then closed the door.

Geonwon had not expected this. He looked at the girl. She was obviously scared.

"Are you okay?" Geonwon asked.

The girl looked at the floor for almost a full minute and then slowly looked up at Geonwon.

He asked her again.

"Why do you care?" she asked in return. "Last week, I was in a camp. Now soldiers use me to…" She left off.

Geonwon tried to hold her. It only made the young girl angrier. She spied the liquor cabinet across the room and slowly walked to it.

"Do you care?" she asked Geonwon.

Geonwon shook his head.

The young girl skipped the glass and took a long drink straight from the bottle.

She sat it down on the nightstand and then began to kiss Geonwon.

CHAPTER 9

The next morning, Geonwon began his new assignment. He was right; it was in China. What he didn't know was how nice the assignment would be.

The food was exquisite. There was a pool for after work. In this time, Geonwon learned much more about coding, hacking, and what the internet was like outside of the DPRK.

Before moving to the base in China, his job had been to fix one of the twenty-six internet sites that officially existed in his country. In China, the internet was almost without limit. Only sites that portrayed China in a negative light were banned.

Geonwon learned what the West believed about his country. The propaganda was laughable at first. One American news source made a fictitious report that all the people in the DPRK were limited to a choice of fourteen different haircuts. Many other false claims were made against his country.

The United States boasted great stores and goods, but his

country did the same. He knew that in his home country, luxury goods were reserved for a few at the top. He was certain that the United States would be similar. He pondered this as he started learning the basics of hacking American social media. He determined that it was highly doubtful that all the things that people had and the freedoms of the United States were true; he assumed they were put on social media sites to trick the countries of the East. Hacking social media was how Geonwon spent his first few weeks.

After a while, he started to believe the propaganda of the West, although it didn't matter to him. His family was well cared for, and he had few worries in a land where hard labor was a fact of life for many of its citizens.

In another six months, he would be up for promotion. When that happened, he planned to buy his mom a refrigerator and possibly a backup generator. Living in China had its perks. You could buy items such as refrigerators and generators on the black market. Shipping would cost slightly more due to payoffs at the border, but it could be done. On a staff sergeant's pay, it could easily be done. In the meantime, he was enjoying some of the best food of his life and working in an air-conditioned hotel in a new and exciting country. They were not allowed to socialize with the locals, but it didn't matter.

It was a dream assignment until on a rainy Thursday morning, his boss, Captain Kahn, approached him at the beginning of his shift. The captain, looking disheveled and frustrated, proceeded to order Geonwon to hack into the government accounting office to hide some of the illegal purchases he had made. When

Geonwon refused, Kahn had Geonwon's family placed in Labor Camp 22.

Geonwon barely escaped imprisonment himself. He was luckily able to outrun one of the elderly soldiers guarding the facility. Geonwon didn't know if the old man was too slow to shoot him or if the ancient guard's rifle was unloaded. He had learned online that many soldiers in his company carried empty rifles, and many ships had sail power only. Fuel was always an issue for the DPRK, which had little money to buy from oil-rich nations.

Geonwon fled the facility and headed north, deeper into China, occasionally checking the government's camp databases. His family members were listed as alive for several months, then their names disappeared. He knew that this meant they had been executed, starved to death, or moved to one of the unlisted camps over the border in Russia. Geonwon considered these options. He didn't know which one would be worse, but the thought of them still alive increased his resolve.

He worked his way through China doing jobs that would make North Korean and Chinese leadership hostile. He showed private citizens how to set up VPNs on their phones and taught them just enough to keep them able to browse freely without attracting too much attention. Tor was a dark web browser that kept people out of the crosshairs of standard monitoring. This was better than the labor that most North Korean refugees could offer. It paid better too.

Geonwon wandered China. He found money and somewhat of a cult status in western China, in the areas that used to be called

Tibet and the areas north of this that were ironically inhabited by Muslims.

He lived well for a man who had the governments of two countries looking for him. But this didn't satisfy him or reunite him with his family.

Geonwon Ku knew he couldn't get his family back with force. If he could find them, he would be killed trying to rescue them unless he could put together enough money to bribe the staff at the camp.

The quest for money led him to reach out to terrorist organizations on the darknet and eventually, work for an unnamed group out of Yemen. His contact reached out to him at a bar in Dubai.

"You can call me Muhammad," his contact said.

"I am Geonwon," Geonwon replied.

"I know who you are and so will everyone else if you don't create a few aliases to use. Our organization will not fail like al-Qaeda and ISIS will fail. You know why? Because they are organized and have titles and the other trappings of a formal organization. I studied in the Americas and Europe. This is what they are looking for. To succeed against a force like the U.S., you need a force that can appear and disappear in the same way that the U.S. defeated the British.

"We are the organization that does not exist. We gather intelligence from ISIS, al-Qaeda, al-Shabaab, and others. We pay for this information in weaponry, but we do not wish to join their cause.

"You are not a pawn in our organization, but an important soldier in an army that is invisible. Read these instructions.

Burn them. Do the job, and then meet me for your payment. Go with God." Muhammad stood and took the hand of a Filipina prostitute. After some negotiation that Geonwon didn't understand, Muhammed left the bar with the woman.

To cause a nuclear meltdown at an American nuclear power plant was a more difficult and gruesome task than he had hoped for, but killing a few Westerners to get his family back would be worth it, he justified.

Then he justified it again. He didn't know if the feeling in his stomach was guilt, hunger, or both.

CHAPTER 10

Doughnuts would be enough food to live on for the next few days if Geonwon succeeded, or even if on the run, but they were a little too sweet for his taste.

What had really attracted him to the doughnut shop was the old-fashioned pay phone outside. He had considered using a burner phone but decided against it. In a town this small, someone might remember selling a disposable phone to someone who looked foreign right before a terrorist attack.

He had purchased a cheap device used to change voices over a telephone and spent a few hours driving around looking for a pay phone. It seemed odd to him that he should make a random list of demands when the result was to destroy the reactor and release radiation into the community, but for eight hundred thousand dollars, he would do as instructed.

Geonwon bought his doughnuts, made his call, and returned to his stolen Chevrolet. He had only a quarter tank of fuel left.

RED HILL

This was not good. He had stolen the car from a laundromat in Illinois, choosing a blue Cobalt because it wouldn't stick out. There were a lot of blue Cobalts on the road, and as luck would have it, another blue Cobalt was parked at a gas station close to Red Hill.

It's time to switch plates. Is it worth the risk? If I get caught switching the plates, the mission is over. On the other hand, if I succeed, and the driver of the other car doesn't notice, my car won't come up as stolen if the plates are checked.

He was just tightening up the last screw in the other car, wondering what the purpose of the small ridges on the side of the screwdriver blade were designed for, when a young woman wearing yoga pants and an orange sweater approached him.

"What are you doing to my car?" she asked, alarmed.

Geonwon froze. *Do I stick the screwdriver in her throat and run for the car? That would attract too much attention.* Considering what he was planning to do, the added pressure of being hunted by the police for murder would not help.

"I'm looking for my phone," he stuttered.

"With a screwdriver?" she asked.

"I just found this here. Is it yours?" he asked.

"No," she replied.

The young woman stooped down to help Geonwon look under the car. He couldn't help but notice the shape of her body in the form-fitting pants and the most likely intentional glimpse of a thong underneath.

"Not there," she said, smiling.

"Thanks for the help." Geonwon walked away as fast as he could without drawing attention.

The whole exchange made him nervous. He knew that he was not invisible, but the idea of having a conversation with someone who might later identify him was unnerving. He drove for another few miles and stole a plumbing van. This would suit his purposes better. White vans with business names on them attracted less attention than even the most common sedans. Plus, the van had the advantages of being able to haul more and conceal the items inside.

Next, he purchased two compact EU-200I Honda generators from an Ace Hardware, two from Menards, and the rest from Lowes and Home Depot. Then he split up the purchases of ten laptops from Staples, Walmart, Office Depot, and two local computer stores. He had siphoned the gas from the van for the generators, but he knew it wasn't enough for the mission.

His next stop was a Love's Truck Stop. He filled the van and bought two additional gas cans and filled them.

The thought of what he was about to do was beginning to upset his stomach again.

He returned to the question in his mind. *Is it better to be remembered as a terrorist or someone who died in a labor camp?* If he could get away, he would be remembered as neither one.

CHAPTER 11

Raymond Church got out of the shower and shaved. Today, he would go to work and operate a nuclear reactor just as he had done yesterday, the day before, and the day before that.

As he splashed the hot water on his face, he pondered about how his life seemed to repeat itself. He had graduated from high school several years ago, and then from the navy's nuclear power school. It was fun and interesting at first, but then it seemed to become tedious. On his last day in the navy, he vowed that he would not be in the nuclear industry as a civilian. Eight months later, his options were fleeting. It was either go back in the navy or try a job in the civilian nuclear program.

Red Hill Nuclear Power Plant was in the small town of Red Hill, only about two hours from his family. So, this was where he dropped anchor.

At thirty-two, he had been married and divorced twice. His first wife Becca had been his high school sweetheart. They were married on his first leave in the navy. Two deployments later, she sent him a letter telling him that she had found someone else. His second marriage was even shorter. He had been on a few dates since then, but none that had translated into a second date. Not a particularly religious man, he wondered if things were preordained, and if they weren't, how he could change them. He wanted out of the nuclear industry, and he didn't want to spend the next year alone.

He then got dressed in his normal work uniform, which consisted of khaki pants, a polo shirt, and brown shoes. This was Raymond's morning routine, complete with toast, half a grapefruit, and black coffee.

As he hit the unlock symbol on his key fob, he remembered what his younger brother Kyle had told him at Christmas. "Tell me which phrase doesn't belong in this sequence," Kyle quizzed.

Raymond had always like riddles, but knowing Kyle, it was going to be something lame.

"Subaru, station wagon, and panty dropper," Kyle continued.

Raymond laughed, but he knew what Kyle was hinting at.

"No wonder you're single. You got to ditch the four-wheel-drive grocery getter if you're looking for women; no woman is going to talk to you driving that thing. You make great money; you should get a Mustang Convertible," Kyle advised.

Raymond considered this for a second, and then thought better of it. Advice or information from Kyle was usually 95 percent wrong, and the other 5 percent was just dumb luck.

"I'll think about it," Raymond lied.

It was now time to stop thinking about panty-dropping

Mustangs and the world according to Kyle. Raymond was almost to the gate where he would go through security, clock in, and assume control of his reactor. Twenty minutes later, after the bored-looking guards, biometric entry procedures, and the customary metal detector search, he was ready to for an uneventful day.

Earl Finn had been running nuclear reactors since the beginning of the U.S. nuclear program. Or so that was the rumor around the control room. Raymond had wished that Earl would retire. Earl had been sliding ever so slightly in his duties in the last few months.

It started a few weeks ago. The reactor had been off a few degrees when he took control of it at the beginning of his shift. He wondered if it had been his fault and ran a trend. The trend came back to read that it had slipped a few degrees sometime around the middle of Earl's shift. Kyle reported this per standard operating procedure, and that had been the beginning of his and Earl's distrust for each other.

"Look, everyone, Gay Ray is here to take charge of the reactor." Earl grinned from ear to ear giving Raymond full view of his perfect false teeth.

Raymond had done his time in the navy as well. Petty homophobic insults weren't going to shake him, even a little.

"Nice shirt, Earl. Does it come in men's sizes?" Earl's wife had died of breast cancer a few years before, which had led to his weekly wearing of the Pepto Bismol–colored shirt that had started to show its age. Not as old as Earl, but getting there.

"Fuck you," was Earl's witty reply.

"You two stop that shit and do your turnover!" Howard Wurtz growled. Supervising this job was stressful enough without these two constantly going at it.

"The reactor has been acting funny for the last few minutes, nothing big, just small changes," Earl announced.

"What kind of turnover is that?" Raymond asked, forgetting about how much he didn't like Earl and looking at the screen with a renewed interest in his usually droll existence.

"Oh, you know everything. You fucking figure it out!" Earl replied.

When Raymond sat down at his station, he started using the mouse, but it didn't work. When he replaced the mouse, that one didn't work either. He quickly notified the duty manager, Bob Felzer.

Bob Felzer quickly went to work investigating the cause of the nonresponsive console. After a few minutes and some curse words that he hadn't used since he was in the navy, he concluded that things were much worse than they appeared.

"We aren't running the reactor anymore. That screen you see is a static screen. Everything on it is going through the motions like normal, but it doesn't mean shit. That's not how the reactor is running," Bob solemnly told them. "We have no control of the cooling systems, emergency stops, emergency diesels, and no idea what the temperature really is."

Howard Wurtz's minor annoyance at shift turnover turned to severe panic as the reality that they were no longer in control of their reactor started to work its way through his body. At first, his feet seemed to be planted to the floor as though his shoes had been glued to it. Then he felt tightness in his chest. *Is it a panic attack or a heart attack? At this point, it doesn't matter which if I can safely shut down the system.*

"Did you try a manual override?" Howard asked, sounding panicked and condescending at the same time.

"Of course," Bob promptly responded.

"Did it work?" Howard was now white-faced and sweating profusely.

Bob looked at Howard with amazement. He thought, *How could someone who has been in this field for so long ask such a stupid question?* It made Bob angry enough to not notice the deteriorating condition that Howard was now in. Bob would have liked to tell Howard a lot of things at that moment, but the gravity of the situation dictated a short, concise response that would allow him to get back to troubleshooting the system.

"No," was Bob's only response.

Howard didn't hear Bob as the heart attack happening in his chest zapped all his concentration. The floor rushed up to meet him before the lights went out.

"Call the emergency number," Raymond said in a matter-of-fact tone to Roy Brighton.

Roy turned to face his console and dialed.

Bob Felzer addressed the control room. "Howard is no longer in charge. I am the senior man in the control room and will be in charge. I'm placing Raymond as acting supervisor since I'm looking at code now to see if I can regain control of the reactor. If any of you have any questions, direct them to Raymond. If he doesn't know the answer, then come to me. Raymond, as supervisor, you're now the incident commander. Notify the city

Emergency Operations Center. I would suggest starting a call-down list and try placing any systems that you may still control in a safe mode. I know we don't have a contingency plan for this, so just do the best you can." Bob turned sharply to the right and headed to the engineering console.

"Yes, sir." Raymond responded and then smiled to himself at calling Bob sir.

Bob Felzer was hard at work trying to determine how to regain control of his facility. The call-down list had been completed, the Emergency Operations Center was aware, and the medics had just removed Howard from the control room, and he was hopefully now on his way to the hospital. *Would it do him any good?* Howard looked bad by the time the ambulance had arrived. Even worse, if the reactor were to have a meltdown, being at the hospital wouldn't do Howard or anyone else there any good.

The phone at Howard's desk started to ring. Very few people had that number due to the high security of the facility. Raymond was now second in command and was communicating with the local Emergency Operations Center. He answered the phone.

"Have you figured out that you no longer are running your facility yet?" a male voice asked.

"Yes. Who are you?" Raymond didn't know whether to be excited or scared.

"Would you like it back?" the voice asked.

"Yes, of course we want it back!" Raymond now figured that the plant was being taken hostage, and something would have to be done to get it back.

"We have a list of demands," the voice replied.

"I don't know what I can do to help, but we'll do whatever we can to meet your demands." Raymond hoped he sounded sincere.

At this point, Bob, who was listening in the background, grabbed the phone from Raymond.

"This is Bob Felzer. I am in charge, and I would like to know what it is that you want."

The voice continued, "No, we're in charge, wouldn't you say, Bob?"

Bob Felzer was about to have his own meltdown.

"What do you want?" Bob asked, trying to not sound angry.

The voice on the other end of the phone paused and then listed a series of demands. "We would like for the freedom fighters in Guantanamo Bay, Cuba, to be released. There are two of our other brothers for our cause who are being held at two black sites around the world. We want them released as well: Yusef Al Hussein and Muhammed Al Yazari. Hussein is at a CIA outpost in Bolivia; Yazari was last known to be in Belgium. Also, you will take Joanne Chesimard off of the FBI's Most Wanted list." The voice paused to wait for a reply from Bob.

Bob did reply with exactly what Geonwon believed would be the response. "I work at a nuclear power plant. I don't have the authority to get you out of a parking ticket, let alone get your friends out of prison or out of hot water with the FBI!"

"You have our demands. Report them to the authorities when you contact them. You now have until noon on November 1 local time to meet my demands, or you will suffer the consequences. If your staff leaves the control room to try to manually activate a SCRAM on the reactor, I'll cause it to overpressurize immediately.

RED HILL

The line went silent. Bob had no idea if the U.S. government would consider meeting these demands.

Geonwon had been tasked with causing a meltdown whether the prisoners were released or not.

CHAPTER 12

George Mendoza was down to his last pack of smokes. He had quit several months ago but had recently taken them back up considering recent circumstances. The Nuclear Regulatory Commission had tasked him this morning with driving down to the Red Hill Nuclear Power Plant. The takeover of the facility had not been reported yet by the news, so when he was called in to his manager's office, he didn't know what to expect.

"You are one of our best inspectors," she had told him.

This made his stomach tighten a little. This conversation was going to be all business. A few months before, he had been a lot more than that to her. His wife figured it out and had taken the courtesy of letting Sharon's husband know. After a few bad weeks at work and one human resources mediator later, they had to agree to avoid each other if possible while human resources contemplated reassigning one of them to a different office.

Both knew that this was where their careers would stagnate. He would be eternally passed up for a promotion when his human resources record was compared with another candidate's, and her glass ceiling was now close enough that she could see her breath in it.

Red Hill wasn't due for another inspection for six months. Surely, they wouldn't just clean out his office while they sent him on a chase for imaginary deficiencies. Or maybe someone called with a complaint. This could be a legitimate concern or some sort of HR office ploy. People were always fired on a Friday, he remembered hearing years ago. This was Wednesday. Nobody gets fired on a Wednesday, he convinced himself.

He then unconvinced himself when Orman Cline walked into the office. "It's time to cut the shit and tell you both what I know." Orman looked like he had aged years in the few weeks since George had seen him. His face was as pale as what corpses usually looked like in the morgue of *Law and Order.*

The last time George had seen him, it was to discuss his interoffice issues with Sharon. That conversation had been unpleasant; this one had the beginnings of one that could be a lot less pleasant.

"Koreans, Russians, Chinese, hell, who knows, have successfully hacked into our reactor system at Red Hill," Orman informed them as he looked at his wingtip shoes. "They have overridden the safety systems, and now our people are no longer in control of the plant. Some assholes from God knows where can cause a meltdown anytime they want."

"What do you want me to do when I get there?" George asked quietly in a voice that was only slightly more than a whisper.

BENSON JACKSON

"I don't know but keep your phone on. My boss just said to send our best guy out there and brief him when he arrives, but hell, I can't do that to you. We could be dealing with our own Chernobyl in our backyard."

CHAPTER 13

"One of the perks of running your own business is that you can run it how you want," Shawn announced before giving a short laugh. He had just opened a cardboard case of Coors Light in the prep area of 5 to 2 Doughnuts. It was almost 2:00, and there was only one customer left in the shop.

"Okay, but keep it down, I'm going to wait until this last guy leaves before I have any," Dave responded.

"You know, for many years, you couldn't buy Coors beer on this side of the Rockies," Shawn commented.

"I know. I've seen *Smokey and the Bandit*," Dave stated in a bored tone.

"Has this guy ever been in here before?" Shawn asked while tilting his head toward the last customer. He then held his head back to finish off his first beer.

"Not that I remember. He keeps asking me if he can smoke in here," Dave replied with a questioning look on his face.

"Well, remind him that it's a doughnut shop, not a time machine back to 1978," Shawn jokingly replied.

David laughed, thinking this would be funny, but the guy looked like one of those management types who worked at Red Hill. Sometimes, those guys would place orders for hundreds of doughnuts. So, pissing this guy off could be bad for the bottom line.

Looking at the man again, he noticed graying temples above a well-worn suit. Then for some reason, Dave pictured the man with a pacemaker scar, barely visible in a Hawaiian shirt, cruising around in a Corvette, looking for women about his daughter's age.

He snapped back to reality and remembered that this guy was drinking coffee the way his grandfather had drunk vodka. It was probably time for a refill.

"Would you like some more coffee?" David asked.

George just stared off into an imaginary world that may have been full of his own version of hungry Bash'em Badgers. David knew nothing of this, so he repeated his question. "Would you like some more coffee?"

"No, no, I'm good. How much do I owe you?" George asked as he pulled out his wallet.

"Twelve dollars and sixty-three cents."

George handed him a twenty. "Keep the change." Then without another word, George got up and walked toward the door.

CHAPTER 14

Governor Irwin Poole was having an odd day. Election Day was closing in, and it was going to be a close one. The challenger for his office was a man named Carl Rothscoat. Rothscoat was about half his age, and most of the people in his state couldn't seem to get enough of him. To Irwin, he looked like someone from a '90s boy band, which made him think of the voters as teenage girls since they were infatuated with most of his public appearances. His day wouldn't have been as odd, except Carl had called him and wanted to have lunch. Irwin agreed, although reluctantly.

Irwin was the first to enter the Candlelight Diner. It wasn't really lit by candlelight; it was an old wooden building from the 1920s that likely would have gone up like a discarded Christmas tree long ago if candles were allowed. He had picked this place due to the knowledge that the food was decent but the privacy was to die for. In its heyday, it had been a favorite for mobsters and others who wanted to go to a restaurant and be seen by as few people as possible.

Once you arrived, one of three waiters would meet you at the entrance and escort you to a booth with its own door. Once that door was shut, the waiter wouldn't come back unless the customer flipped a switch that illuminated a light on the outside of the booth.

Irwin had been here many times before. When his mother was dying of cancer, he would meet a local guy, who went by the mononym of Cal, at this restaurant. Cal would supply Irwin with high-quality marijuana. He never once felt guilty about purchasing the substance, but he knew that he would be removed from office if anyone knew. There was no way that legalized marijuana would happen in this state anytime soon. It was too risky to send one of his staff, although most would have done it.

Looking over the menu, he couldn't decide on what to have. The cheeseburger was sub-par, and the chicken fingers weren't half-bad. Before he could decide, Carl entered the booth.

"How are you doing?" Carl asked enthusiastically.

"Not bad. And yourself?" Irwin answered and asked with a smile and shook his hand.

"I'm doing fan-fucking-tastic" was Carl's reply.

Irwin hadn't expected this type of meeting. Carl seemed almost in a state of complete bliss, the feeling that marathon winners, lottery winners, and in general, life's other winners get to enjoy only on special occasions. Irwin hadn't been that ecstatic when he had won the governor's race.

"It's interesting that you picked this place, Irwin." Carl's grin reminded Irwin of a saying that his grandfather used that involved possums eating strawberries. Irwin thought that no matter what Carl was talking about, there was not much of a chance of him knowing why he normally came here.

"You've been a bad, bad boy, Governor Poole."

Irwin had learned to play poker at an early age, and his face was not about to give anything away.

"Tell me, Governor, when you get the munchies, do you order a big basket of fried mushrooms?"

"I don't know what you're talking about," Irwin stoically replied. There may have been some rumors leaked somewhere, but rumors were part of most politicians' lives, he figured. His face gave away nothing as he mentally tried to figure out where the rumors could have started.

"I won't make you try too hard to figure out how I know," Carl started again. "You see, my cousin is a hospice nurse. Your mom was a cancer patient. Is the picture getting clearer now?" Carl flipped on the light to summon the waiter without taking his eyes off of Irwin. "You know, you could have probably had some intern get your shit for you with just the promise of a better job. Then if he'd have ratted, you could have just called him a liar."

"What makes you think that I won't just call you a liar when you go public?" Irwin asked.

"Pictures of you and your convicted pal Cal arriving and leaving here around the same time and a few of your mom using God's herb."

Irwin was furious but knew that anger would not make the situation better. He thought that coming to this restaurant was the safest bet for these transactions, but he never gave any consideration to the fact that people, as well as other customers, might be watching him in the parking lot. Rothscoat had figured his little secret out, and now it was time to go into damage control. He was still trying to figure out how he could try to intimidate Carl into not blackmailing him when his phone rang.

"Ooh is that your meth dealer?" Carl asked sarcastically, his eyes looking down at Irwin's phone.

Irwin's mind flashed to a multitude of scenarios where he could somehow kill Carl or blackmail him first when he spoke into the phone. "Hello."

"Governor Poole, this is Al Holder, Mayor of Red Hill. We're in serious trouble, and we need you down here right away!"

"What is it?" Irwin asked, feeling the urgency through the phone.

"Someone has hacked into Red Hill Nuclear Power Plant and has given us a list of crazy demands," Al said with a shakiness in his voice that made Governor Poole uneasy.

"Okay, I'll be there as soon as I possibly can," Irwin responded as he hung up the phone.

Carl listened as intently as he could, but the only words that he was sure he understood were the words "red hill."

"I'll deal with you later, but if you go public with those pictures, you might have a tough time living long enough to be a governor." It was an empty threat, and Irwin knew it, but Carl might not. Either way, he didn't think it would stop Carl too long.

Carl considered this threat over the beer he had ordered. He thought about it some more over the beer that Irwin hadn't bothered drinking, and even more over five additional bottles that he ordered after that. His mind began to wonder. Irwin didn't have the muscle or the spine to kill another human. He started to think about this as another thought entered his head. Why didn't he just google "red hill" to see what was happening? He dropped his phone on the first try, but then with some steady determination, turned it on.

Carl didn't have to google anything, as the last thing he had looked at on his phone was the news. It had since updated when the presidential race was the main story.

"Trump vs. Clinton" had been replaced by an anxious-looking reporter standing by a sign that read "RED HILL NUCLEAR POWER PLANT." The headline read "Unknown Group Hacks Red Hill Nuke Plant, Gives Demands for Return of Control."

Carl clicked on the link and watched a young reporter give a grim account of the details from the scene. A soberer Carl would have figured that the best strategy would be to watch the events unfold and very publicly critique any mistakes, or even perceived mistakes, that Irwin made handling the situation.

But this was the Carl who felt invigorated by the checkmate he had set up earlier, and now fueled with a little liquid courage, decided that after a few more drinks, he might just go down there and show the governor up. There would be a lot of cameras, potential voters, and just bystanders, who would witness Carl acting as a far-better leader in times of crisis.

He ordered another drink and began to let his mind wander as it often did after a few. He barely remembered his parents.

They died when he was a child. Would they have been proud of him if he became the governor? Would they be proud of him if he failed? His father had killed his mother with a 12 gauge shotgun and then had turned it on himself.

He often found himself wondering why he cared about the thoughts of two long-dead people. Had they not met such an early demise, he might not have ended up living with his uncle Ira. Ira made Carl kill many of the animals they ate. A confirmed bachelor and raging drunk, Ira often abused Carl and told him that if he ever told anyone, Carl would die just like the pig whose throat Ira slit on Carl's first day at his house. These vivid memories made Carl want to cry until he remembered how Ira met his end.

Ira had many pigs on his farm, but the one that never made sense to Carl was the wild hog that Ira had captured in the woods. This hog was large, aggressive, and angry. Ira aptly named him Hell Hog. He would often throw smaller animals in the pen with Hell Hog just to watch him kill and eat them. It was a morbid sort of sport for Ira that horrified Carl.

One day, at the ripe old age of thirteen, Carl, as best as he could tell, became a man. It started out like any other Monday. He went to school, where he was often teased and made fun of for his clothes. When he got off the bus, Ira was yelling for him from what he thought was the hog house.

When Carl walked into the hog house, Ira wasn't there, so his voice must have come from behind the hog house where Hell Hog lived.

Ira had taken a pitchfork to Carl's favorite barn cat, which Carl had named Oliver. Ira was now holding Oliver's impaled, bleeding body over the fence for Hell Hog to devour. The cat wiggled just a few times as its life was escaping its body. Hell Hog stepped forward eagerly and began sniffing at Carl's only friend.

Ira scraped the cat off of the pitchfork against the fence and started to chuckle as he set the tool down. He then started looking for the bottle of whiskey he had brought out with him. He hazily pondered why he wasn't hearing the sniffles of a child. Carl was a timid child and would surely cry for hours after the loss of this cat.

Carl's first reaction was shock, then warmth as another feeling crept through his body. It seemed to rise up from his feet, a primal, powerful feeling that he had never felt before, and would feel only a few times afterward in his life.

He watched as Ira struggled to find what he assumed was his bottle of whiskey. Sloppily, with his back turned to Carl, he almost stumbled as he found what he was looking for on the step of his old tractor.

Carl heard the cork come out of the bottle and watched as Ira turned his head back to take a large drink of the substance. It would be his last. Carl took the pitchfork from the fence and rammed it through Ira's back.

Ira screamed as he tried to turn around to face his attacker, but Carl held the handle with a firm grasp. The handle flexed in Carl's hands as the wood began to splinter. Ira tried to shout something at him with his dying words, but Carl didn't understand him.

Ira's knees buckled after what seemed like an eternity. He coughed and spat blood onto the tractor.

RED HILL

Carl picked up the bottle of whiskey off the ground and took his first drink. It tasted better than he thought possible. When the alcohol entered his bloodstream, his mind began to clear. He had watched his uncle run the old Farmall tractor many times. It had a dump bucket on the front.

He climbed onto the machine, careful not to touch the blood. It was starting to turn black, which contrasted clearly from the red paint of the tractor.

After a few minutes, he had it running and started to experiment with the controls. Shortly after, he had scooped up Ira's corpse with the bucket and started to creep toward the pen where Hell Hog lived.

It took Hell Hog almost a week to eat Ira.

Carl grieved at first. Then he felt triumph. He had faced his fears and knew that he could now do anything he wanted. If anyone got in his way, they would face the same sort of fate as Uncle Ira.

These thoughts, while always in the background, came and went. They were starting to fade now as Carl remembered how far he had come since his youth. He celebrated this fact over several more drinks.

CHAPTER 15

Twenty miles away, the same news story was airing over the sales counter at Shoot'Em Up Gun and MMA Supplies. Tank Porter and Bill Reilly were closing Shoot'Em Up for the day, maybe forever. There were still some customers outside beating on the glass doors. They could have sold as many guns today as they had in the whole time they had been in business. But Bill had convinced Tank that if they didn't get out of here, they wouldn't live long enough to enjoy it.

Both men had trained in MMA and worked out frequently. Neither one of them possessed the skills that would ever make it to the professional ranks, but with their fighting skills and access to so many weapons, they had learned to enjoy the ability to intimidate anyone who wasn't a paying customer.

As they got into Tank's lifted Dodge truck, the conversation changed direction.

"How far should we go to avoid this shit?" Tank asked.

"I don't know. I wish we had some of that Prussian Blue that they were talking about on the news," Bill responded.

"What the fuck are you talking about?"

"It's a pill you can take to block the effects of the radiation to your thyroid." Bill answered staring out the front windshield.

"What?"

"It was on the news," Bill trailed off.

If there was anyone who intimidated Bill Roberts, it was Tank.

"I've seen that shit!" Tank exclaimed. "Remember when we went to Bull Creek Military Surplus?"

They had broken into Joe Reece's store last summer to steal some of the inventory and try to force him out of business. But when they got there, there were just a few guns and a bunch of old army stuff. They figured it wouldn't be long before he went out of business on his own.

"Are you sure it was Prussian Blue?" Bill asked.

"Yeah, I just figured it was some sort of shit to make meth with, but there were cases of it in the storeroom. Let's go there and take that shit!" exclaimed Tank.

"Maybe it would be safer to just drive away from the radiation," Bill replied.

"Maybe you can just fucking get out and walk away from the radiation; I'm going to Bull Creek and take that Russian shit," Tank angrily replied.

Tank drove while googling Prussian Blue. He had never heard of Prussia before and didn't know if it was close to Russia or not. That would be another google search for the future.

CHAPTER 16

A few miles away, Carl Rothscoat slid into his green Camaro. He rarely drove at a high rate of speed or even wanted a sports car, but his wife Helen had insisted that he needed a young, fresh image. The aging Ford pickup that was more favorable to his current budget would not present the image of a younger man coming into power.

Carl had to be careful. If he was pulled over by the local authorities, his bid for governor would now be over, but the chance to show up Governor Poole was too great of an opportunity to pass up.

He considered texting Helen to let her know about his great idea, and then thought better of it. It was the type of idea that was likely to start a fight at the Rothscoat household. In Carl's mind, if he took a risk and succeeded, he was the hero. If he took a risk and failed, life around the house would be rough for a while.

He dug his phone out of his pocket, deciding to turn it off so that Helen couldn't call him if she saw him on the news.

Carl dropped his phone. While fumbling for it, he managed to run a stop sign and pull out in front of a lifted Dodge truck.

Tank managed to swerve enough to just clip the front of the Camaro and then slam on the brakes. After what seemed like an eternity to both men, the truck finally came to a stop. Bill wanted to check on the driver of the other car. Tank told him to shut his mouth and dropped the shifter back into drive. Unfortunately for Tank, something in the crash had damaged the shift linkage. The truck was stuck in park. After a few cuss words and a few punches to the dash later, Tank agreed to check on the other driver, or at least steal his car if it would still move.

Carl Rothscoat reached down between the seat and the center console. When he had bought the Camaro, he had removed the tire iron from the trunk and placed it the passenger area of the car. He had taken a few shortcuts in life. He grinned despite himself. *Sometimes shortcuts create enemies,* he thought. If he couldn't talk his way out of this, he might create some more enemies today.

There was no movement from the green Camaro until they got about ten feet from the driver's-side door. Carl Rothscoat emerged from the car trying his best to appear sober.

"Sorry guys, I dropped my phone." Carl hoped to get his bluff in early.

"You smell like a damn brewery!" Bill replied.

"I'm running for governor; I just came from an important lunch meeting." Carl hoped they would buy this story.

"You're running for governor? You should be running from me," Tank said, preparing to punch Carl in the face.

Yelena Harris was leaving the hospital. She had just finished a sixteen-hour shift and was thankful to finally be driving home. The coffee in her mug was starting to upset her stomach. She rolled down the window and tried to pour it out, but the wind blew it up her sleeve. Thankfully, that same wind blowing in from the outside started to wake her up some, so she left the window down.

She skipped through the radio stations in her Forerunner, and not wanting to hear what was on either classic rock station, she had another groggily conceived thought: *Classic rock is awesome; why isn't there more of it?* Then her mind went down a rabbit hole that concluded that if it was new music, it couldn't be classic rock. She kept switching the stations and eventually stopped on the news. The local drudgery of small-town news peeking out between national headlines had been replaced with something that awakened her from her almost automatic drive home.

"Red Hill Nuclear Power Plant appears to have been hacked from outside of its facility. It's too early to provide details, but stay tuned to WWKL, your local news source, as coverage will continue until we get answers."

The voice sounded urgent, but not fearful, she thought. Maybe with good reason. Surely, nuclear power plants had all kinds of safeguards and ways to safely shut down the plant manually in case of an incident.

RED HILL

The voice on the radio returned: "WWKLP has just learned from an unnamed source that if a list of demands is not met by noon on November 1, then the perpetrators of this act will intentionally cause a meltdown of the reactor at Red Hill. If this occurs, WWKLP will sound the emergency alarm to notify its listeners of the attack and provide instructions."

"Holy shit!" Yelena exclaimed.

She gripped the wheel as though she might bend it and contemplated her next move. As a Red Cross volunteer, she didn't know if she should contact them for instructions or report back to the hospital. If something happened at the plant, she might be needed there.

Then her sense of self-preservation kicked into high gear. *Maybe getting the hell out of here might be a better idea.*

Yelena started taking stock of her life up until this point. She was a fraternal twin. Originally from Minnesota, she had gone to college near Red Hill and had moved back there after her divorce. Her twin brother, Steven, had joined the Marines at seventeen and was wounded in Falluja. She often thought about the fact that they had been so close as children and had shared so many of the same experiences, except that he had shed blood for his country and would always be a hero in their family. While she had gone to college and was doing well in her profession, she never dreamed of doing anything that might seem that heroic. Maybe today would be the day! She considered this.

Another thought flashed back to her. As a child, her great aunt Ida would watch her and her brother for her mom after school. Ida would often toast marshmallows for Yelena and

Steven over the gas stove. They smelled wonderful, but often, Ida would keep them on too long and turn them into something that resembled charcoal. Yelena pondered if the same fate awaited her if she stayed in Red Hill.

Those thoughts were at odds with each other when she made one of the last turns before coming to her house and almost ran into a parked green Camaro that looked like it was missing some pieces. There were two men in glittery MMA shirts. These were often the type of men she had seen in the emergency room. Usually, it was for the types of injuries that homeowners often face, such as falling off ladders or muscle strains. But what made these types of men more noticeable was that they often came in with unusual injuries.

She tried hard not to stereotype these men in her head, but many of the strange and frankly stupid injuries that she had seen in the last few years were conducted by men in tight shirts with fighting slogans on them. The dumbest that she could remember were two rednecks testing bulletproof vests on each other. Only 50 percent of the test must have been conducted, she grinned, because only one of the two men in the ER that night had broken ribs.

As she eased her car closer to the Camaro, she could see the truck that must have hit it. The two men in T-shirts were shoving a familiar-looking man in a suit.

She eased her car a little closer to the group and was sure; these were the men from the bulletproof vest test.

Yelena stopped her car a few feet from the Camaro and rolled down her window. "Is anyone hurt or need medical attention? I'm a nurse." She said this loud enough to hopefully discourage the two-on-one fight that looked almost certain outside of her car.

The larger one of the two looked at her and said, "You also have a car."

She now recognized the man in the suit as the guy running for governor, Rothscoat or Wainscot. The adrenaline rush from the radio announcement and car wreck was wearing off, and she was starting to become drowsy.

The two guys from the ER and the politician were arguing loudly and talking about something called Prussian Blue. He promised them the first dose if they'd forget about the wreck.

Yelena was almost asleep when the three men approached her car. Rothscoat's veneer smile seemed to fill her driver-side window.

"Good morning. I'm Carl Rothscoat. You may have heard of me; I'm running for governor. There has been an emergency at the Red Hill Nuclear Power Plant. I was hoping that you could give me and these two fine gentlemen a ride to the scene. I know it may sound like a lot to ask, but in the event of nuclear contamination, there is a medicine called Prussian Blue. I'll make sure you get one of the first doses if the need arrives."

Yelena hit the unlock button on her Forerunner. The three men quickly jumped into the car. Yelena moved the transmission selector to drive and then hesitated. Looking in her rearview mirror, she was startled to see a military convoy rapidly approaching.

The first truck slowed down slightly to swerve off the road to pass the wrecked cars. The second and third trucks followed suit. Truck number four attempted the same maneuver and blew its driver-side front tire. When it lumbered back onto the pavement, the driver pulled over to the right shoulder, allowing the rest of the convoy to pass. The final truck in the convoy pulled up behind the one with the blown tire.

As Yelena pulled past these vehicles, Carl noticed the emblem on the back of the truck read "CST." He immediately started googling. "Those guys are the CST!" he cheerily read from his phone.

"I read that off the bumper. What the fuck does that mean?" Tank growled.

"They're a full-time National Guard Unit that responds to mass chemical attacks and nuclear attacks. This is great!" Carl exclaimed.

"What's great about it?" Bill asked. "As a matter of fact, if we must use them, we're hosed. What do you think they're going to do? Put a cork in a reactor and then spray some magic army dust to decontaminate us?"

Carl ignored this. Mentally, he was already shaking hands with army guys in front of army trucks in front of the first TV camera crew he could find.

CHAPTER 17

Shawn and Dave were just finishing up a case of beer. 5 to 2 Doughnuts was cleaned and prepped for the next morning. Dave's phone sent him an emergency alert. Most of the emergency alerts were about missing people from the surrounding states. This one read:

POSSIBLE TERRORIST ATTACK AT RED HILL NUCLEAR POWER PLANT. RESIDENTS OF THE SURROUNDING AREA ARE ENCOURAGED TO EVACUATE THE AREA.

Shawn had just finished sanitizing the sink when his phone gave the same message.

"Let's go, Dave!" Shawn was running for the door, keys in hand.

"I don't think that will be an option," David trailed off.

5 to 2 Doughnuts was located on Norman Street between the Red Hill Nuclear Power Plant and the town of Red Hill.

Norman Street was completely full of cars. It was normally a two-way street, but today it ran only one way. Police, fire, and military vehicles were lined up in one direction, heading west to the plant.

The option to drive away had passed. It was over a mile to town, and after gathering a few things, they would still have to walk or thumb a ride out of town.

"What do you think, Shawn?" asked Dave.

Shawn had military training. He was also more creative and had figured out a lot of the hurdles that almost blocked 5 to 2 Doughnuts from becoming a reality.

"We can't leave here, at least not in the car. I have the four-wheeler out back. We could drive the shoulder back into town." Shawn's expression suggested that he was deep into a planning session.

Dave knew that Shawn was planning something crazy, but Dave's adrenaline was up, and he would go along with whatever crazy plan Shawn was concocting.

"Hear me out," Shawn began. "You know who Ron Tepper is?"

"Yeah, the rich old bastard who owns the fuel oil business," Dave answered.

"Well, his sons run it now, but my grandpa told me how he became rich." Shawn paused for the dramatic effect as well as to make sure that he had Dave's undivided attention. Then he continued. "In the 1970s, there was a gas shortage." He paused again.

"Yes, and shitty disco music," Dave said flatly.

"Yes, but shitty disco music aside, there was a fuel shortage. Tepper Fuel went from an operation with two trucks and three employees in a one-room office in the back of a gas station to what it is today, by taking advantage of the fuel crisis." Shawn knew he was going to have to explain more, but Dave looked ready to interrupt.

"By lowering prices and eating the losses?" Dave asked.

"No, by establishing a very low interest program and by never refusing to fill a fuel oil tank on someone's house, no matter how long it had been since he had been paid. This bought him the loyalty of everyone in this town who used fuel oil as a heat source. It hurt him in the short run. He lost his house in '78 and his wife in the process. Grandpa said that for a while, at the leanest point, he even lived in that office in the back of the gas station. But the fuel crisis ended. He remarried another woman. His third son went to college to become an accountant, to help run the business."

"Who uses fuel oil anymore?" Dave asked again, not seeing the significance of an outdated product in the wake of nuclear winter.

"Okay, some of his other kids studied heating and air. They install all kinds of furnaces and central air units. That's a moot point in what I'm talking about. What I'm saying is that no one in this town over forty will use anyone else for fuel oil or another heating and air company due to the loyalty and relationships that they established back when Carter was in office and that shitty disco music you were talking about was still popular."

Dave believed that Shawn had something more profound than fuel oil and air conditioners on his mind, but he didn't quite know what.

Shawn continued. "We can't leave town even if we want to. Odds are the government or the army or somebody will stop anything bad from happening. This means if we give away free doughnuts to people who are stuck in traffic or just walking through town, they'll likely remember us as a business that cares about this community. So maybe we die in a miserable radiation-induced death. Or maybe that doesn't happen, and we build a brand loyalty for doughnuts that the grocery stores will never be able to touch. We lose a couple of hundred dollars' worth of product, but build a relationship with the community that turns us into the only place that locals will even consider for doughnuts. Maybe we'll be able to franchise. Turn the fryers back on. I'm going to fuel up the four-wheeler and hook the lawn trailer to it. We'll use all of the dough we have to make as many as we can, and then we'll ride into town to distribute them."

"I'm not riding bitch on the back of your four-wheeler!" David proclaimed and then laughed out loud.

"If you keep drinking beer like that while making the doughnuts, I'll have to pour you onto the back, doughnut bitch!" Shawn was laughing now, imagining Dave wearing a tiara and handing out doughnuts to passersby.

CHAPTER 18

Hanna Green heard the news in her car and texted Cindy to cancel their plans. *I have to get Taylor and get him as far away from this as I can.* Of course, this will be the first instinct of every other parent in town.

She made it into the school quickly, but a wreck on the way out of town slowed their progress. Taylor was scared; Hanna may have been even more scared but was determined not to show it.

She wanted to find some soothing oldies or jazz music on the radio. All she found was static. Hanna could feel a panic attack coming on but didn't want Taylor to know. She wanted to lie down in the street until it passed. When the attcks happened, lying flat in a quiet place was the only way that she had been able to stop them in the past. This was not an option today.

Driving away didn't look like an option yet either. Hanna looked out her window at something she had driven by hundreds of times without really noticing. It was an army surplus store. *Should I buy some emergency supplies? If nothing else, it might entertain Taylor until the traffic clears.*

Hanna and Taylor opened the door to the very crowded surplus store. The gun case over the counter was almost empty. In the front of the store behind the counter was a very somber-looking older man dressed in an old army uniform.

The shop felt very small and humid. She didn't know if this was due to all the customers today or the preferences of the elderly sole proprietor. She could hear and feel the wooden floorboards creak when she walked across them, and she smelled shoe polish and the hot smell of starch after it has been seared by an iron.

She held Taylor's hand to keep him from getting lost in the crowd. The group of people in the shop were trying to yell over each other to tell the old man what supplies they would like to buy. Some were trying to make trades with him for cars and other things that would be useless if the town became another Fukushima.

The old man's uniform had a name tag on it. Hanna was almost close enough to read it when he picked up a megaphone and screamed into it. "Listen up!"

The sound from the device in that small of an area was almost deafening. The noise of all the would-be customers fell silent. Joe set the megaphone down on top of the glass counter and proceeded to address the room in a briefing that Hanna considered calm, given the events of the afternoon.

"I have meals ready to eat, or MREs, that I'm going to pass out to the women and children first along with some water purification kits. When that's done, I'm willing to make a deal on the few remaining items in the store. I have some emergency medical supplies such as Prussian Blue that may help people survive in the event of a meltdown, but seriously folks, I think the safest thing for all of you to do is to get in your cars and get out of town. Radiation can't harm you if you're far enough away. If you're determined to stay or you just want some MREs to eat while travelling, form a single-file line in front of the counter, women and children first. After they have their rations, we can conduct any remaining business deals."

Joe finished his speech and began opening a cardboard box filled with brown bags of field rations as the line started to form in front of the counter. There were very few women or children in the room.

Hanna and Taylor were the second group in the line. The first woman in line looked like she was maybe just old enough to drive, except for the tattoos that she had on her neck and arms. The old man put three MREs, a canteen, and a box of water purification tablets in a bag for her.

As Hanna waited in line, she couldn't help but wonder if the shelves were almost empty due to the scare, or if this wasn't a very profitable business to begin with. The conversation between the young woman and the older man, whose last name was Reece per his name tag, interrupted her thoughts.

"I want some of the radiation pills," she growled at him.

As Hanna was now much closer to Reece, she could sense a certain sternness and sense of authority that the military had instilled in him and that age hadn't taken away.

Joe politely but forcefully told her, "The pills are for survivors if there's a meltdown, for those who for some reason couldn't make it out. I doubt that it'll come to that, so like I said, take these supplies, get in your car, and get out of here. *Next!*"

The young woman scurried away as though she was used to getting what she wanted and would surely write a bad review of the place online, if she lived that long.

Joe was already filling another bag as Hanna approached him. When he noticed Taylor, he put three extra MREs and another canteen in the bag.

Taylor was looking in the glass case at a compass. "Can I have this?" he asked his mom.

Before she said no, Joe interrupted. "You might be a little young to read a compass, but do you have a watch?"

Hanna frowned at the thought of the omnipresent badger watch of Taylor's that was missing for some reason today.

"No," he said.

"Then I have just the thing for you!" Joe said with a warm smile.

Beside the compass in the glass case was a box of army-looking green watches, each with a Velcro strap.

Hanna couldn't tell if Taylor was more excited to get a gift or if Joe was more excited to explain the gift to him.

"I'm going to write down the instructions on this piece of cardboard on how to use an analog watch as a compass. Once you master that, you'll always know where you're going and what time it is. Those are both good things to know."

"How much?" asked Hanna.

"Don't worry about it. I figure this place will get looted five minutes after I lock the door and leave. Plus, this will give you an activity if you get stuck in traffic or have a lot of downtime in the next few days," Joe handed them the bag.

He had obviously had children in his younger years and knew the value of keeping them busy, she thought. He placed the piece of cardboard in the bag before they walked away.

"Thanks!" Taylor said with a smile, already putting on his new watch.

"No problem. Next time I see you, I want you to be able to find directions with it," Joe said.

Joe and Hanna both hoped that there would be a next time.

CHAPTER 19

Frank Coleman was making good on his promise to clean the gutters for Janice. The sun had come up and was starting to make the job a little more bearable. The gutters had some pine needles and a couple of pine cones, but not enough to stop the flow of water.

Frank started to believe that this job was just to provide peace of mind for Janice. Perhaps she had an unreasonable fear of the gutters freezing. But he suspected something more. He had noticed that Janice rarely had any visitors.

Cleaning gutters, mowing, and doing a few small repairs didn't bother Frank. As a matter of fact, retirement had been a dreary experience for him. He travelled extensively in his working years and had no desire to do the same in retirement. He didn't have an interest in fishing or hunting. About the only activity he enjoyed was target shooting a couple of times a month. However, helping Janice had other perks. Conversation, for one. She was one of the few people he interacted with anymore, and she never let him go hungry.

Frank was stepping off the ladder when Janice opened the door. She brought him out some biscuits and gravy.

"How's it going?" asked Janice.

"Not bad, I should be done in a little bit, and then I was going to run to the store. Do you need anything or want to go?" he asked.

She didn't get a chance to answer. They both turned to look at the road. A rumble was coming from the west.

Janice and Frank lived on a small two-lane road. They stared off to the west to see a pair of headlights and then another. Ten military trucks drove by, and then the two-lane road was quiet again.

"The Guard is a long way from the freeway. I wonder why they were driving by here," Janice said.

"That wasn't the National Guard," Frank replied.

"No?" she asked, observing the confusion in Frank's face. "Who do you think it was?"

"CBIRF," he almost asked.

"What's that?" She was now very curious.

"CBIRF is the Marine Corp's chemical biological unit. I did some training with them about five years ago in Indian Head, Maryland. They're active-duty Marines. They respond to large-scale chemical, biological, and nuclear incidents. They augment the local response efforts. What they're doing here, I have no idea."

Frank walked over to his car and turned on the radio. They listened to the announcement in silence.

CHAPTER 20

The emergency operations center in the basement of the Red Hill Police Department was activated shortly after the event began. It started with just a few key members.

Sheriff Tim Baylor unlocked the room and turned on the lights. Within the first half hour, the liaison officer, public information officer, safety officer, and section chiefs arrived. Additional staff continued to arrive in the first hour.

When the last of the Emergency Operations Center staff had reported to their station, Tim gave the team a briefing. "Attention, everyone. The Red Hill Nuclear Power Plant has been compromised. You may be wondering what that means. From the information that we have now, it means that a hostile entity has taken it over. The operators and engineers for the facility are no longer in control. They're trying to regain control of the facility, and we do not yet know if they'll be successful. The Nuclear Regulatory Commission is sending an advisor. His name is George Mendoza.

I don't know how much he'll be able to do, given the situation. I feel it necessary to warn you. If we cannot regain control of the reactor, we won't be able to survive in this Emergency Operations Center for very long. Command will fall to the State Emergency Operations Center in that occurrence. I just want to be up-front with you that there is a very real possibility that we could all die. So, I won't hold it against you if any of you want to leave."

Tim paused to see if anyone would take him up on his offer. He hoped that some would. No one got up to leave. He was surprised at the amount of civic duty or possibly bravado the staff showed by staying.

He continued his brief. "We know what the terrorists want but are in no position to offer it. Two of the people they want freed do not show up in a google search, so I have no idea who they are. The third is someone who murdered a police officer and fled to Cuba. I have no idea if the federal government will cooperate," Tim finished and looked around from person to person.

"Sounds like bullshit to me," replied Deputy Kepler. "There is no way the government is going to release those people, and if they do, not in that short amount of time."

Tim ignored him and continued. "As you all know, we have made announcements for people to clear the area. But as in the flood of '08, we can't force people to leave. Our public information officer is now here. So that is how we communicate to the outside world. No rogue texts. Everyone knows or will soon know the gravity of the situation. Traffic to Red Hill has been blocked. State police are letting a few members of the press enter but no one else. The main road leaving Red Hill is Interstate

70. The latest report has a fuel tanker overturned, blocking the on-ramp to the interstate. Crews are working on moving this and redirecting traffic to alternative routes out of town."

Tim was interrupted by his deputy announcing the arrival of George Mendoza. The two men shook hands and walked to the incident commander's area.

"How is this possible, and do you have a plan to stop it?" Tim quickly asked.

"The complexities of how they hacked into the facility would take a while to explain. This is obviously a sophisticated operation. It would take a very gifted hacker or group of hackers and several computers," George explained dryly.

"That's good to know, but that's almost obvious. How do we stop them? They could be halfway around the world." Tim was beginning to wonder if the addition of George Mendoza to the team would be of much help.

"Yes, that's possible, but the probability is low. It would be difficult to verify what control you have without being able to physically see what you're doing. It would be a huge risk to contact the plant and tell them what you're going to do unless you were sure you could do it. For instance, if I were doing this, I would try to set up somewhere close to the plant so that I could monitor some small changes or run some tests. The most obvious would be to remotely move one of the cameras or open a security gate remotely. Once you can verify that you've gotten that far, you can continue from there. I've been there before. The facility is isolated per design, but what are some of the other buildings or businesses around? Think of those with lots of computers or just lots of empty space that could be used to set up in. An abandoned store? Anything?" George asked.

"There's a library that's being remodeled. It has a computer lab. Lots of computers, but it's filled with construction workers. It's highly doubtful that anyone could work in there without being noticed," Tim said.

"The person or group would just need a clear line of sight or someone in the plant to verify that the commands being given would happen in the field. I want a satellite photo of the area," George stated.

"We don't have satellite imagery; all we have is Google Earth," Tim replied.

"That's fine if there hasn't been any new construction since the last update. This is your town, Sheriff. Has there been any new construction in the area?" George asked.

"None in the area. I'll get you that map," Tim offered.

George instinctively reached into his pocket for a cigarette. His pocket was empty. He walked over to the coffeepot and made his eighth cup of coffee for the day with powdered creamer.

Tim returned with the eight-by-ten picture of the surrounding area. The library was visible in the northwest corner. To the south, there was a strip mall.

"What's in this strip mall? Is it still open?" George asked.

"Just a few small stores. There used to be a Sears Hometown Store in the middle, but it's empty now," Tim replied.

"That's the first place I would look. With a scope, you could see the plant from there. Send some cops over there, whatever you have."

CHAPTER 21

Geonwon vomited into the floor for the second time. His stomach was heaving. This store was supposed to be his operations center for only a day or two. He had used the bathroom at the Happy Hoosier Motel before checking out. There was no electricity, other than what his generators supplied, and no running water. He used the an open area of floor a few feet away from his computers as both his bathroom and trash can.

He had set up his shop in an abandoned Sears. The doughnuts had been too sweet and were making him feel woozy. He found some microwave popcorn and an old Zenith microwave that had been left when the store had closed. The salty popcorn had tasted wonderful. Geonwon ate the whole bag as soon as it came out of the microwave. Ten minutes later, he was vomiting. The popcorn had expired in 2003.

At the same time Geonwon was vomiting out his expired popcorn, Bob Felzer was heating up a can of soup. Bob knew from years of experience that sometimes, a few minutes to relax and let his mind wander might bring a new solution to mind. Bob had trouble letting his mind drift. He knew he might die and that the land his family lived on for four generations might become a radiated wasteland, but what bothered him more was that he didn't know whether either of his kids had made it out of town.

In all of the years that Bob had trained for an incident, most of the drills involved what was called a SCRAM, which makes a meltdown impossible. The only problem now was that the SCRAM was impossible. There was no control from inside the control room, and the knowledge that the terrorists could control the CCTV system and cause a meltdown before anything could be done in the field put him in a state of panic.

He had just eaten his first bite of soup when he heard the unmistakable sound of a helicopter landing just a few hundred feet from the control room. About thirty seconds later, there was a loud knock on the door.

Bob peered through the plate-glass porthole and saw an identification badge that had the letters "FBI" on one side. Bob opened the control room door.

"Agent Petrov, FBI," Petrov said, extending his right hand.

"Bob Felzer," Bob replied while shaking his hand. "You know you took a hell of a risk coming in here. The guy on the phone said he would go ahead with overpressurization if he saw us leave the con. He didn't say anything about helicopters, but I'm going to have to assume he meant that as well,"

Petrov flashed a weak smile. "Do we even know if they have this capability?"

"It's my belief they do," Bob replied.

"I dropped in here to assess the situation on the ground. I'm not a reactor expert, but one named George Mendoza will be here shortly. I honestly doubt he can do anything that your people can't, but Incident Command is about to cut all communications within twenty miles. You're going to want this." Agent Petrov handed Bob a radio. "I have a few soldiers outside who are looking around for anything suspicious, but it's doubtful they'll see anything. When they finish their sweep, we'll be on our way. This radio will allow you to communicate with Incident Command. We also brought you some MREs." Agent Petrov paused. "Additionally, the event is way too big for Red Hill. Incident Command is now in Indianapolis. I know you know how important this is. Even the president is wishing you well as he tries to do some CYA."

"So, radios and phones are going down?" Bob asked.

"Yeah, and CBs as well. But Incident Command has a sense of humor. They're playing some old '50s song on some AM channels on a loop. The nickelodeon song," Petrov said with a slight grin.

"Why?" Bob asked.

"I don't know. Psychological warfare maybe," Petrov replied.

Bob frowned and put the MREs on a table.

A soldier knocked on the control room door and pushed the intercom button.

"Exterior is all clear, sir," the soldier announced.

"That's my cue. If you need anything, just radio it in," Petrov said as he exited the control room and made his way back to the helicopter.

Bob ate his soup cold, not talking to Raymond Church or anyone else. He looked at the radio, wondering what help they could be, and then an idea crossed his mind.

There might be a way to override what the hacker had done, but only if they didn't think through all of the support utilities for the plant. Red Hill's reactor was set up to automatically shut down in a safe configuration if grid power was lost coming into the plant. The standby diesel generators would kick on and keep the facility operational for maintenance and cool the reactor, but this was an off-normal condition, which should cause a safe shutdown. Bob didn't know who comprised the Incident Command Center, but he hoped they were the kind of people who could make things happen.

Bob picked up the radio and started to speak. "This is Bob Felzer, duty manager at Red Hill Power. With whom am I speaking?"

"This is Incident Command Operations Section Chief. Go ahead," the voice replied.

"I would like you to cut grid power coming into the plant. That might help; it certainly won't hurt," Bob replied.

The lights flickered for only a second, and then the diesel generators kicked on. The control screens told him nothing. There was a red light that was set up on analog control that could be used to verify when the reactor went into a SCRAM. It didn't illuminate. The reactor controls continued to run on diesel power.

Bob knew that whoever hacked them was skilled, but they must have also researched the reactor and plant design. The diesel tanks were large enough to run the plant for several weeks.

"It was a good idea," Raymond Church said.

"Would have been a lot better if it had worked," Bob replied.

CHAPTER 22

The Forerunner carrying Yelena Harris, Carl Rothscoat, Tank Porter, and Bill Reilly arrived in town shortly before the state police barricaded the entrance to the town. Governor Irwin Pool had beaten them by half an hour.

Traffic was filling the town square of Red Hill. Carl Rothscoat noticed Irwin Poole's Cadillac in an alley. He hopped out of the Forerunner, with this parting phrase of "Thanks for the ride, and don't forget to vote!"

"Hey! He promised to make sure we got the Prussian Blue medicine," Yelena yelled. She wasn't sure if she was yelling at Carl or her two passengers.

"I'm going to kick his ass!" Tank growled as he reached the door handle.

"Stop!" Bill yelled. He calmly explained to Tank, "That guy is basically a used car salesman. I doubt that he can get us medicine. We might not even need medicine if we can get out of here. We're almost past the square. The interstate isn't but about ten miles from here. Fuck that guy. Fuck his probably nonexistent medicine. I'm just glad that Yelena is giving us a ride. Let's keep going."

Tank usually gave the orders. But this time, he couldn't think of a single good arguing point. He wanted to beat Carl into a pink puddle on the sidewalk, but Carl's first move was to run into an alley just a few yards from the police station. Tank didn't want to deal with police. He didn't want radiation poisoning. He released the door handle, happy to put as much distance between the power plant and himself as he could.

Yelena didn't know what to think of her passengers. One was a violent, short-tempered man. His sidekick seemed more like a tagalong, but Bill was the brains in the relationship. She recalled that night in the emergency room. It was Tank who had been on the receiving end of the bulletproof vest test. The idea of travelling with these men made her uneasy, but she was exhausted. She knew she couldn't make them leave her car. She assumed they knew that as well.

She had been looking in her rearview mirror since Tank had grabbed the door handle. A knock on the driver-side window startled her.

"Free doughnuts!" Shawn Graves exclaimed.

Yelena rolled down the window, and Shawn handed her six doughnuts.

"Thanks! "Yelena said.

"No problem!" Shawn exclaimed. "Remember, 5 to 2 Doughnuts is your one-stop post-apocalyptic doughnut shop!

Take care and safe travels!" He walked away and started knocking on other cars. Yelena didn't know if she should laugh or be scared. She checked her phone to see if the hospital had called her back, but there were no messages, and she had zero bars.

She handed four doughnuts back to Tank and Bill, who quietly devoured them. "I'm very tired. Could one of you drive for a while?" Yelena tried to fight back a yawn but was unsuccessful.

"Sure, I'll drive for a while," Bill replied.

Bill and Tank both moved to the front. Yelena moved to the back. Traffic was still not moving when she went to sleep.

Governor Poole was finishing up his meeting at the Emergency Operations Center and briefing the public information officer, Lana King, on exactly what he wanted to say to the press.

"Thanks again for doing this, Lana. I'll give another statement later, but if you can get this information to the networks, then hopefully we can inform the public. I know that the police and public works are trying to clear a path for people to exit the city, but I know that some of them have fled as well. I don't blame them." Governor Poole finished with a handshake and turned left to walk back to his car. Lana turned right to go meet the local press.

Governor Poole had parked his Cadillac in an alley a few yards from the police station. On the short walk back to the car, he noticed an act of random kindness, two twenty-something men who were handing out free doughnuts.

His phone buzzed. He reached into his pocket. It was a text from his wife. He made a mental note to answer it later.

He reached back into his pocket for his keys. When he had entered the alley after seeing the doughnut giveaway, he had been alone. But he felt the presence of someone else behind him. Did Lana want to go over some more interview material with him? He turned around to see Carl Rothscoat.

"What are you doing here, Carl?" Irwin asked through clenched teeth.

"Oh, I think I'm going to become governor today." Carl looked disheveled. His tie was crooked, and he walked the zombie walk that suggested that he may have stayed at the restaurant drinking well past their earlier meeting.

"What do you mean? The election is in three weeks!" Irwin could no longer hide his anger.

"Well, the lieutenant governor's in the state capital today, right?" Carl asked.

"Yes," Irwin replied.

"I plan to release a statement to the press when I have assessed the situation. The people will see me in charge…"

Irwin interrupted. "That's not how it works. This is an emergency. The public information officer briefs the press. This is not a political shit show. I may not win reelection, but I am not going to let the people of this community be subjected to your smoke-and-mirrors show in the middle of a crisis." Irwin was shouting now.

Carl looked over his shoulder and scanned the alley. "Oh, I thought about speeding the election up," he muttered with a half-smile.

"What do you mean?" Poole confusedly asked.

Carl began again. "Well, if you were to die, say, by one of the terrorists, then I run unopposed. Given the fact that I'll take command of this situation here and your lieutenant's in Indianapolis counting pencils, he would be stupid to even enter the race."

Carl reached into his jacket with his gloved right hand. When his hand reemerged, it was holding the tire iron that he had slipped into his sleeve.

"You drunken bastard!" Irwin shouted.

Carl lunged at Irwin, swinging the tire iron over his head. Irwin put his left arm up to block, but the force of the tire iron shattered Irwin's ulna. He tried to fight Carl off, but it was no use. Irwin started going into shock upon observing his left arm. Somewhere between the elbow and the wrist, it was turning an ugly color, and he could feel the bone starting to protrude from the skin. All the while, Carl was hitting him across the face and then on the side of the head. Irwin fell to his knees, and in a last-ditch effort, punched upward, catching Carl in the groin.

Carl doubled over, but it didn't stop him. Irwin tried to stand up again to run, but he staggered and fell. The younger man was on top of him in a second, pressing the sharp end of the tire iron into his throat.

"Say hello to the future," Carl hissed as he drove the tire iron deeper into Irwin's throat.

Irwin struggled and began to gargle. The last thing that he noticed was the smell of alcohol. His body went still.

Carl dumped the tire iron into the storm drain and began to stagger slowly to the police station.

CHAPTER 23

Roper Thompson heard something about evacuating the town. He didn't know quite where he had heard this or why people were leaving. He only knew that he was feeling worse. He needed something he could steal and quickly convert to cash.

There was a line of cars heading out of town. Guys were handing out free doughnuts. He didn't want food. He knew he wouldn't be able to hold it down. He didn't like being seen; besides, it was hard to steal stuff when there were a lot of people around.

He walked into an alley where he used to buy weed, but his old weed guy wasn't there. Instead, there was a dead guy and a car.

Roper stooped down to look at the man who appeared to have bled out from his throat. It was hard to sell a stolen car, but he might be able to find a chop shop. It would be difficult but possibly more lucrative than just pawning a few stolen tools.

The keys were in the dead man's pocket. The picture of the man in the license looked familiar, but Roper couldn't place him. The corpse on the ground didn't look like the picture at all.

Roper took the cash from the wallet and dropped the rest. He planned on hiding the car for a few days, then driving it to Indianapolis. He would have to be careful to not be spotted, or he could be blamed for the dead guy on the ground.

This might be a good day after all.

Roper dropped into the driver's seat and admired the nice interior of the car. This car might fetch more than he originally thought. He looked in the console. He knew a middle-aged guy with a car like this probably didn't have anything like heroin or meth, but maybe he kept a bottle of bourbon or vodka to spruce up Roper's morning.

The glove box surprisingly had the answer to his quest. A Ziplock bag full of weed and some Zig-Zags was setting on top of a road atlas.

Roper lit up and pulled out of the alley straight into a slow-moving lane of traffic. He was smoking weed in broad daylight in the middle of his small town. Ordinarily, he might expect to be arrested, but the people all seemed to be leaving as fast as they could. They paid no attention to Roper driving a car that he could never afford, let alone smoking weed.

Whatever apocalypse shit show was happening, it was making Roper's day. He stopped as he was leaving the town square. The Shell station was empty. Roper grabbed a case of beer, some beef jerky, and walked back to his car. Then he thought that if no one was here, he might as well press his luck. He went back in and took all of the scratch-off tickets as well.

Back in his Cadillac, he fought the urge to completely fill the car with gas station snacks. Beer and beef jerky in the park seemed like a better idea. He had been arrested at this park twice, but today it would be empty.

He looked out at the bridge over the river. In the distance, he could see army trucks driving in a line. Roper didn't know that they weren't the local National Guard. He wondered if life would have been different if he could have joined the Guard, done his twenty, and maybe used the GI bill to go to college.

As he finished this thought, the hand-rolled cigarette started to burn his thumb. Then he laughed, believing it was much easier to steal stuff out of storage buildings.

Carl walked up the steps of the police station. The two young men who had been driving around on the four-wheeler approached him.

"Free doughnuts!" Dave shouted.

"Thanks!" Carl replied.

When Dave extended the tray to Carl, the self-proclaimed governor grabbed the tray with both hands and ripped it out of Dave's hands.

"Hey!" Dave yelled.

"You said they were free!" Carl screamed as he turned around and sprinted into the police station.

"What an asshole!" Dave proclaimed.

"Yeah. I wasn't going to vote for him before and definitely not now. Come on," Shawn said, "let's go. We still have plenty of doughnuts to hand out,"

Carl Rothscoat expected to hear busy phones, police talking to witnesses, and an almost Black Friday atmosphere when he entered the Red Hill Police Department. Instead, he opened the plateglass door to see Deputy Anna Ford by herself, reading a magazine. She looked up immediately and asked him if he needed assistance.

"I'm here to see the sheriff," Carl replied.

"He's in the Emergency Operations Center. I'll call him," Anna offered.

"Where is the Emergency Operations Center?" Carl asked.

"In the basement," Anna replied without thinking and then thought maybe she shouldn't have told him this, but it was too late.

"He'll want to see me," Carl muttered as he rounded the corner to a door that read "Basement." He twisted the handle on the door, and luckily it opened. He didn't know if Officer Ford would have allowed him in, so he continued.

Officer Ford saw no reason to call the sheriff. If Sheriff Tim Baylor didn't want the guy there, he would throw him out.

Carl staggered down the stairs to the Emergency Operations Center. The stairway smelled strongly of disinfectant and was dimly lit. He almost lost the tray of doughnuts once. He could not do that. His whole running platform up until this point was that he was running as Santa Clause. He wouldn't let that image be tarnished. No car wrecks, dead opponents, or dimly lit hallways were going to spoil that for him.

He steadied himself and grabbed a doughnut. Maybe a doughnut would disguise the smell of beer on his breath.

Carl knocked on the door of the Emergency Operations Center. A young deputy, who looked like he had just finished high school, opened the door. "This is the Red Hill Emergency Operations Center," the deputy announced. "State your name and your purpose for being here."

Carl looked down at the young officer whose name tag read Kepler. He could push past the officer and maybe bullshit his way in, or it could get ugly, and he could be arrested. Carl was a pusher. This determined his course of action.

Carl pushed his way past the young man as the officer reached for his Taser.

Carl panicked. "Stop, officer! Don't you dare Taser me! I am the governor-elect, and I demand to speak to whoever oversees this operation now!"

"Don't taze him, bro," Baylor said, hoping that everyone would know the reference. If they did, they didn't find it funny. He looked at Carl, sizing him up. "I'm Sheriff Tim Baylor. I'm also the incident commander for the Red Hill Emergency Operations Center. I don't think you can quite call yourself the governor yet. The election is weeks away. I'm sure my staff will appreciate the doughnuts, but I am curious as to what you're doing in this room, and even more curious about the blood spatter on the collar of your shirt. Furthermore, I want to assure you that I am in charge of this incident until relieved. You do not have any authority here. So again, I will ask you, where did the blood on your shirt come from?"

RED HILL

Carl's bloated face showed less emotion than someone who was considering repaving his driveway or maybe putting some new orchids in his office before a meeting with a member of the press. Inside his head, however, was a sudden realization that his bid for governor might end with a lifetime sentence in federal prison. Instead of the governor's mansion, with young interns to spend time with, he might end up spending time in an eight-by-eight cell.

One of the key elements of his campaign had been prison cuts. "Too much is spent to feed and clothe these people," to quote one of his cost-saving initiatives. He pondered the irony of those cuts taking place if he were caught.

A scary new realization came across Carl Rothscoat. It seemed to come up at him from the floor like a cold windless draft, turning warmer as it reached his throat and then his temples. Killing Irwin Poole was not done out of necessity. Carl had a comfortable lead over Poole in the final three weeks before the election. Carl could even blackmail him with the marijuana purchases. If the buying of illegal drugs by Governor Poole were somehow leaked, the election would have been over.

Killing Irwin Poole had been an act of complete mastery and domination. He had rarely considered killing another human since his uncle Ira, but this time, it had felt wonderful. Carl believed that somehow, he gained the power of the people he killed. He was not so sure that he wanted to govern them anymore, as much as he might like to kill a few more of them.

The more he thought about it, he knew he wanted to kill someone else. He didn't have anyone in mind, but he was certain that at sometime in his life, sooner than later, he was going to need that rush again.

The draft he had experienced earlier, that somehow burned while giving him chills, had subsided. He knew it was time to bullshit these people for all he was worth.

"That's why I said governor-elect. Governor Poole and I were strategizing over what do about this situation when we were attacked by the terrorists."

"What?" Sheriff Baylor almost screamed. "What happened to the governor?" Baylor prodded. "You've seen the terrorists? Who are they? Where are they?" Baylor was shouting now.

George Mendoza stepped in close enough to the group to smell the alcohol radiating off Carl. "Okay," he interjected. "What can you tell us about the terrorists? Are they Middle Eastern, American? Russian, Chinese? How many of them are there?" George was trying to piece together the situation.

"I don't know. They were wearing masks," Carl replied.

"What did they say? What were they driving?" Tim Baylor now chimed in. He was hopeful about the resourcefulness of Mendoza, but this was a police matter, and he wasn't about to let Mendoza do the questioning.

"Again, they were wearing masks, four or five of them. They didn't speak. It's all kind of fuzzy. It was a horrific experience." Carl was hoping he could draw enough sympathy from the two men to be above suspicion.

"Is Governor Poole okay? Where the hell is he?" Baylor had also noticed the aroma of beer emanating from Carl.

"I think he's dead," Carl answered somberly.

"We need to know what happened, and you need to start talking now." Baylor was quickly losing his patience with Carl Rothscoat.

"They stabbed him in the throat with something," Carl replied. "That's the last thing I saw before I blacked out. They hit me over the head with something."

Carl didn't want to say too much. He knew that too many details could lead to the sheriff calling bullshit on his story and could possibly mean he would have to recall all of these details again later.

"Do you need medical attention, Mr. Rothscoat?" Baylor asked. Carl's story wasn't completely convincing him, but he wasn't sure why.

"I understand that you were hit on the head and are probably in shock from what you've seen, Mr. Rothscoat, but it is really important that you tell me where this happened and when," Baylor continued.

"About ten minutes ago in the alley between the empty storefront and the army surplus store." Carl had made no attempt to hide the body nor could he think of a good reason to lie about the location.

"This happened ten minutes ago, and you stopped at the doughnut shop four miles down the road before you got here?" Mendoza asked.

"No, I bought them off the guys selling them on the street on the way in," Carl replied.

"Excellent! We finally caught a break," Baylor remarked.

George Mendoza had no idea why the location of the murder was a lucky break.

Carl immediately broke out into a cold sweat. He didn't know why it was a lucky break either, but he intended to find out.

"Mr. Rothscoat, you're sweating profusely. We have a medic that can examine you. Wait right here, and I'll get her." Baylor started to look for the medic when Carl started to protest.

"I'm fine," he stated. "I want to help you catch who did it. Plus, I need to be here for the people. The governor is dead, and the lieutenant governor is in Indy. I may not be governor yet, but I need to be here for the people." Carl's sweat had run from his forehead to his now-soaked shirt.

"The alley you're talking about is the alley between the old Hook's drugstore and Bull Creek Military Surplus," Baylor noted.

Carl and Mendoza were silently waiting for more of an explanation from Baylor. Mendoza couldn't figure out if the sheriff was pausing for dramatic effect or if there was something that he didn't want Carl to hear.

Carl could feel his heart beating in his ears. The sweat running down his back had now settled in the crack of his ass. Unpleasant, he mused, but not as unpleasant as prison.

"Last year, someone, probably teenagers, broke into Bull Creek. They broke a bunch of stuff but didn't steal anything of value. Anyways, Joe Reece owns the place. He's in the Citizens on Patrol Program, which is also known as the pain in the ass to the real police program. He insisted that a camera be installed on the roof of the police station to be pointed at his store after hours. The town council wasn't going to pay for it, but since he paid for the camera and monitor, they let him do it. We need to go to the top floor. We can look at the footage, and hopefully, that will give us an idea of who we're looking for." Baylor opened the door to the Emergency Operations Center and sprinted up the stairs.

Mendoza and Carl followed.

Three floors later, the three men were breathing heavily. George Mendoza cursed at himself under his breath for smoking most of his adult life.

Tim Baylor was pushing one of the seemingly endless supply of keys on his ring into the door handle.

Carl Rothscoat was silently hyperventilating. The smell of antiseptic had penetrated deep into his lungs. That smell, combined with the running, foggy malaise of drinking all day, and his first murder in many years, had now made Carl's stomach start to churn.

The second brass key on Tim's key ring opened the door. As the three entered the room, somehow Carl believed that the antiseptic smell had gotten stronger. *So help me God, if I become governor, I'm going to ban the use of this shit in all gvernment buildings*, he thought.

Tim Baylor moved the mouse, and the screen of the Dell desktop lit up.

Carl Rothscoat could no longer hold the mixture of doughnuts and beer in his stomach. He lurched over the trash can and vomited from what felt like the bottom of his feet to the back of his throat. He tried to lift his head to see the monitor, but his eyes had filled with the blurry tears of a good vomit.

He wiped his eyes with his sleeve and vomited two more times. He was ready for a fourth, but he held it in. Wiping his eyes one more time, he looked around the room. He had no idea how he would explain it or what he would do after, but he had made up his mind—George Mendoza and Tim Baylor could not leave this room alive.

He thought briefly about what story to tell the police after it was over and came up with nothing. *First things first*, he thought.

The room was little more than a janitor's closet. Ironically, there were no large bottles of green disinfectant to be seen. Carl scanned the room again looking for any sort of a weapon. The sheriff's back was to him and a large black handgun was on his hip, but a gunshot would attract too much attention.

In May 1995, the first woman sheriff of Red Hill, Bridgette Sheppard, had won the Kelly Parker Second Annual Golf Scramble. She succumbed to pancreatic cancer eight months later. Bridgette was a widow when she passed without children. Her replacement was Tim Baylor.

When Tim moved into her office, he spent the better part of an afternoon cleaning out her effects. They didn't amount to much, he thought at the time. Most of her stuff was just office supplies. He tossed most of them into the big Rubbermaid trash can in the breakroom. The one item of hers he could not throw out, and yet didn't want to have as a daily reminder, was her trophy from the golf scramble. He had moved it to the third-floor closet that was now the Citizens on Patrol meeting room.

Carl Rothscoat now held this trophy in his hands. Tim Baylor was rewinding the footage. The screen was fuzzy in rewind, like an old VCR. Per the time stamp in the lower left corner, he was closing in on the only footage of the murder of Irwin Poole.

RED HILL

Carl had formed his plan. He would bash Tim Baylor over the head and then do the same to George Mendoza. He would then steal the recording and destroy it. Carl didn't know if he should go back to the Emergency Operations Center and take command afterward or try to leave town. He really didn't know what he would do next. *First things first,* he thought again.

"Here we go," Tim Baylor said, staring intently at the screen that stopped flashing and cleared up.

Carl had only moved the trophy up to chest level. He expected to see himself on-screen murdering Irwin Poole. Instead, the camera was filming the flower shop that was three stores east of the alley.

"Shit!" Baylor screamed. He continued to scroll through the footage from the two previous hours until now. The camera had been pointed at the flower shop the entire time. Irwin Poole was on film walking toward the alley. Carl wasn't on the recording anywhere. It showed two men giving away doughnuts to stranded motorists and passersby.

"Did you say you bought those doughnuts?" George Mendoza asked Carl.

He answered by asking, "Who is Bridgette Sheppard?"

"You are an asshole governor…excuse me, governor-elect" replied Mendoza.

"Never mind who the hell Bridgette Sheppard was," growled Baylor. He was in no mood to give a history lesson.

"Well, what happened to the footage?" asked Mendoza.

Baylor looked down at his hands on the desk. "My deputy, Kepler, is infatuated with Caroline Reedy. She's the daughter of

Charlie and Simone Reedy. They own the flower shop. He must have been up here camera gazing at the shop. I ought to fire that dumb fucker but not until this is over. We're short-staffed as is. Either way, I don't see your terrorists, Mr. Rothscoat, so hopefully my men will find something at that empty Sears store."

To use the term "breathed a sigh of relief" would be an understatement for Carl Rothscoat. He knew that he wasn't in the clear, but he no longer needed to murder two more people and try to cover it up. He might even get away with killing Poole.

His sweating started to subside. The stench of the almost certainly green antiseptic wasn't even bothering him anymore.

"Well, I don't think we'll accomplish much more up here," Carl said with a new sense of confidence. He now felt almost as good as when he had been blackmailing Poole. But he didn't feel as good as he did from their meeting in the alley.

CHAPTER 24

Hanna Green had not made it as far in her journey as she had hoped. Five miles from her purchases at Bull Creek Military Surplus (she had also bought a flashlight and a flint fire starter), she ran into a traffic jam. People were outside of their cars. Some appeared to be tailgating. There were barbeque grills, a couple of bonfires, and a surprising amount of beer for a group of people who were fleeing for their lives.

Hanna told Taylor to stay in the car and then locked it with her key fob a total of three times before checking the handle just to make sure. The first person she ran into was a man wearing a pair of black jeans and a wallet chain. A crucifixion T-shirt completed the ensemble. His brunette hair was worn in the style of the man bun, which Hanna believed was the mullet haircut of this generation. This was not the type of guy she was hoping to run into.

"Hello," the man offered a simple greeting.

"Hello," Hanna returned.

"There's a semi or something overturned on the on-ramp, so there's no telling when we'll be able to leave. Hopefully, we'll be able to leave before anything bad happens at the nuke plant. I've been listening in on my CB," he shared.

Hanna thanked the man before returning to her car.

"Hey!" the man called out. "Would you like something to eat?"

Hanna didn't know if the man with the wallet chain was just another harmless traveler or something more sinister. But she decided to return to her car and not find out. She hit the key fob as she glanced at the car. Taylor was nowhere to be seen. Hanna's anxiety, coupled with possibly losing her child, caused her knees to buckle. She braced herself against a sycamore tree and began to scream.

"Taylor!"

"What?" Taylor yelled from a picnic table in a small clearing just a few feet from the road. The tattooed lady from the army surplus store sat across from him, and a large pizza from the Texaco gas station laid on the table between them.

Hanna sprinted over to Taylor. "I told you to stay in the car! What are you doing over here?"

"I was hungry," Taylor replied. He knew that he wasn't supposed to go anywhere with strangers, but he had already seen this lady today, and she had pizza. So maybe she would be okay, he thought.

"Relax, lady," the tattooed woman mumbled. "I saw you both at the army store earlier, and I figured you might like something better to eat than those shitty army rations."

Hanna had left her neighborhood in a panic. She had packed water, clothes, and the toothbrushes but had hoped to make it out of town before they needed food or the army rations.

"Me and my brother got four of them from the gas station. Have some." The tattooed lady held out her hand at the pizza. Hanna was starving. She sat down beside Taylor and grabbed a slice of pepperoni and green olive pizza. As she started to eat, the young woman began to speak again.

"I'm Kara Felzer. My dad works at the nuke plant and texted me and my brother Troy when whatever happened went down. He didn't say much except for us to get the fuck out of town," Kara explained.

"Watch your language around the kid!" Troy hissed as he approached them from the road.

Hanna suddenly felt rude. She had almost run from the young man that she now knew to be named Troy Felzer, and here he and his sister were sharing what may be the only food they have. Even more crazy, the man-bunned, wallet-chained young man was even concerned about language around Taylor.

"Hi, my name's Troy. I didn't get a chance to introduce myself earlier." He shook Hanna's hand.

"Hello, my name's Hanna, and this is my son Taylor. Thanks for the pizza."

"No problem," Troy returned.

"What are they saying on the CB?" Kara asked Troy.

"Well, the army's blocking all exits out of town. There's still a fuel truck overturned, and the public works department is trying to move it at this on-ramp, but when you get past that, the army is blocking the interstate. They're also blocking all of the backroads out of town, so I don't think we're going to be able to leave."

"Well, why aren't you still listening to the CB in case the army gives instructions or something?" Kara asked.

"For one, I'm hungry." Troy sat down beside Kara and grabbed a slice of pizza. Before he took a bite, he said, "Also, the CB's no longer working. I thought it might be a fuse, but the fuses are fine. I don't know why it isn't working unless the army is using a frequency jammer. The only reason I can figure they're blocking the road is that they're hoping the terrorists or whatever are inside city limits. Hopefully, they're not the religious-extremist type. Maybe if they're stuck here, they won't destroy the reactor." Troy stopped talking long enough to take a large bite of pizza.

Hanna had almost forgotten about Beau. He had gone exploring through the woods. Tiring from the exploring and soaking wet, Beau trotted back up to the table and stood on his hind legs. She didn't think that pizza would be too good for him, but dog food was another thing she had forgotten in the haste to leave.

She tossed him the crust from her second piece.

CHAPTER 25

Geonwon finished vomiting into the drying puddle of urine he had left between the empty store racks. He was finished setting up his program, which set in place a course of events that would cause the reactor at Red Hill Nuclear Power Plant to overpressurize, releasing radiation into the atmosphere. He verified his work and walked outside.

He had used almost all of his fuel to run the generators. There was one and a quarter cans left in the back of the van. He picked up the quarter can and poured it into the gas tank. He kept the other one in reserve and placed it into the van beside his remaining laptop.

He slid into the driver's seat of the van, not sure if he would vomit again or not. He started the van but left the door open. When he was sure his stomach had settled, he closed it.

Taking one last look at the power plant in his side mirror, he knew there was no going back. He was a terrorist, and if he didn't get out of here soon, he would have killed all those people for nothing.

Geonwon placed the transmission selector in drive and fought the urge to drive recklessly out of the parking lot. Timothy McVeigh was only caught due to a traffic stop, he remembered. If Geonwon was caught, it was not going to be for something as stupid as speeding. His original plan was to take the fastest route to the interstate.

His GPS said he had five miles to the interstate when he came upon a sea of cars parked on the road between him and his escape. Geonwon tried to reprogram the GPS for another route, but the GPS was no longer functioning.

Bob Felzer and Raymond Church had exhausted every avenue they could think of to regain control of the reactor. Whoever had hacked their facility wasn't just good enough to take over the facility, but skilled enough to make sure that the engineers at Red Hill could not regain control.

A few people remained in the control room to do what they could, but Bob had texted his children and let them know to get as far away as they could from Red Hill before communications were cut off.

Bob hadn't given up on stopping the meltdown, but his hopes were dwindling. This had caused him to reflect on his life and family. His legacy was two twenty-somethings named Kara and Troy. Troy had planned to join the navy just like his father, but he didn't pass the medical entrance exam. He had an issue with his inner ear that could be corrected by surgery. Troy had the surgery, but by the time he had healed, he had lost interest in the navy.

Bob had offered to pay for Troy to go to college for anything he wanted to do. He hoped his son would pick something with computers, but in an odd turn of events, Troy had picked the ministry.

Bob and his ex-wife Sarah had never been the religious type. He could count the number of times he had been to church on one hand. One of those times was to get married. They had taken Troy and Kara to church a few times when they were very young for Sunday school. Bob often wondered if those mornings had a profound effect on Troy, given his choice of college.

Kara was different. She had made exceptional grades all through school. Bob had little doubt she would begin college and have a great career after high school. She did not. She could never explain why, but in the two years since her graduation, she had done little except work a few hours a week at the Texaco.

Bob made a promise to himself that if he made it through this, he would get to the bottom of why she had very little interest in school or a career. But that would have to wait for another time. If he didn't make it out of here alive, he at least hoped his kids would.

Raymond Church had called his family as well. They lived a few hours away, although not completely out of harm's way, depending on the wind direction. Luckily, they were west of Red Hill, which meant for now at least, they were upwind.

"Who do you think would have done this?" Raymond asked.

"Well, in the good old days, you could have laid money on it being the Russians. But hell, who knows now? North Korea?

Iran? What makes things worse is that the U.S. has software to blame it on whoever they want to. If this was done by the Saudis but the government wants to invade Iran, they'll blame it on the Iranians and invade. Whoever did this was sophisticated, but nowadays, there are many hackers who could do something like this. We may never know. Could be radical jihadi. That's who I think it is, but again, could be anyone."

CHAPTER 26

Frank instructed Janice to pack enough food and supplies for a few days. She protested, but he told her he would explain when he got off the phone.

For many years, he had been called upon for emergencies. He felt strange now being on the other end. His call to the fire department didn't connect to the Red Hill Fire Department. Instead, after a slight delay, his call was answered by dispatch in Indianapolis.

Frank had called to volunteer to return to the fire department, but not being able to talk to the local chief Gary Ames, he decided to get Janice out of town and return to see if he could be of help. He knew that the local 911 system was supposed to switch to a digital system that would transfer calls to another fire or police station in a situation where the local station's communications were down.

He then tried to call his nephew Jerry Kepler, a new deputy in the Red Hill Police Department, but his phone was no longer working. He tried Janice's landline. It wasn't working either.

RED HILL

She had just returned to the kitchen with what looked like an ancient suitcase. "I brought some of food and my medicines, but I don't think any canned goods will fit."

"That's okay," Frank said. "If for some reason we can't make it out of town, we may have to hole up here."

As they walked to his truck, he tried the phone one more time, but it didn't have any signal. He placed Janice's suitcase in the bed.

After they drove off, he tried to find updates on the radio. The only noise coming out of it was static. Frank stopped trying to adjust the radio due to the heavy amount of traffic in the town square. The two guys who owned the doughnut shop were handing out free doughnuts. It seemed like an odd gesture in the current situation, but kind.

Janice continued to search through the radio stations as Frank focused on the stalled traffic. She found one that still had static but with a hint of music.

Frank turned up the volume as far as it would go. He listened intently as the sound faded in and out. He hoped that it might be the emergency broadcast station.

Traffic had come to a standstill. Frank killed the engine and put his finger up to his lips to give Janice the shush sign. He then turned his head to the right to put his ear closer to the radio. He grinned slightly when he thought about how silly this was; the sound was coming out of the speakers in the door.

He sat back up in his seat. It no longer mattered. He knew what the sound was. It wasn't the emergency broadcast system, nor was it any sort of news. It was a song from 1950 called

"Put Another Nickel In" by Teresa Brewer. He wasn't born until 1955, but it had still been popular in his youth.

"What is it?" asked Janice.

"Just a song; unfortunately, a very bad one at that," Frank replied.

"What do you think we should do?" she asked.

"If traffic doesn't start moving again, we're going to have to walk back to your house and do as much as we can to seal off radiation. It's not ideal, and it may not even work, but this truck is almost no protection at all. It would shield us from alpha waves just fine. But the beta and gamma rays would go right through the metal and us." Frank almost whispered the last part.

"Looks like traffic is starting to move again." Janice smiled.

"We can go left at the other side of the square and try to go north, but it might take us longer that way. If there's a meltdown at the reactor, we need to get as much distance between us and it as we can. I think we'll just hit the interstate," Frank stated as he went straight at the end of the town square.

Two cars behind Frank and Janice sat Joe Reece in his ancient Jeep Scrambler. His Ford Ranger had its final muster last week. Luckily for Joe, he had been working on his Scrambler for the past few months. He could do some of the work himself, but some of the heavier work he farmed out to the Red Hill High School auto shop. He was leery of letting high school kids work on his classic Jeep, but after seeing the job they did on the transmission, combined with the fact that some of them took payment in army surplus goods, made them his go-to destination when he needed shocks, a radiator, and the rear differential rebuilt.

RED HILL

Joe had loaded down the bed of the truck with MREs, jerry cans of water, ten cases of Prussian Blue, and some ammo. He had a tent and some sleeping bags in the cab. He wasn't planning on living in the woods, but he figured if the store were looted in his absence, he would have the most valuable of his remaining merchandise with him.

Joe tried to tune in the radio. He twisted the ancient knobs, only to hear static. He thought he heard a trace of that old song about putting nickels in something called a nickelodeon. *If that's the only thing on the radio, then maybe it's better that it doesn't work.*

He switched over to the AM band, and after a few more minutes of static, smacked the dash. If this whole thing blows over, he would run it into the high school and see if the kids could fix his radio.

Traffic had stopped again. Just as well, Joe mused. He was a little behind today on his vodka intake. He reached under the seat and brought out his lucky canteen and took a healthy swallow. It didn't really burn going down anymore. He wondered if that was good or bad and almost failed to hit the brakes when the car in front of him stopped. Joe attempted in vain to honk the horn, but no loud honking came from the engine compartment. *Add horn to the list of things to have fixed next.*

Traffic started to move again, and that was all right with Joe. He wanted to get as far away from Red Hill as he possibly could.

His hopes of putting distance between himself and Red Hill dwindled five miles out of town. He drove around a corner to see a makeshift camp of stopped cars.

Joe took another swig from his canteen before he let the reality set in that be would be camping here.

CHAPTER 27

The dedicated line between the Red Hill Emergency Operations Center and the State Emergency Operations Center rang. Sheriff Tim Baylor picked up the receiver to be notified that the Red Hill Emergency Operations Center was to evacuate.

He commanded the remaining officers and volunteers to get as many people as possible into each car to cut back on the traffic congestion. Baylor wanted to find out what his officers discovered at the abandoned Sears store, but he was told to call them off. The State had informed him that this event was now being considered interstate terrorism and that the federal government was now in charge. Their orders had been to place a cease and desist order on local law enforcement. Baylor didn't like this, but he complied.

George Mendoza also talked to the State and told them about his theory. He was told that they would take the information into consideration, but it was highly unlikely that an attack would be launched from a local location.

Mendoza pleaded his case. "You don't even want us to send a couple of guys over to check it out? If it's being run out of there, all we need is a deputy to unplug the computers, and hopefully arrest the terrorists!" he screamed.

The voice on the other end of the phone replied, "If you or any deputies set foot in that store or make any attempts at apprehending the suspects before the feds arrive, you will be held liable and tried in a court of law for any radiation release."

Mendoza hung up the red phone in the room. On the other end of the line, Geonwon closed his laptop and began smashing it with a rock.

"Trying to order another pizza?" Cindy Peller asked.

Geonwon froze. He had no idea that someone was that close to him when he put the call through to the Emergency Operations Center. It was the lady from the hotel. He had bypassed the army's jamming technology, which would have made him the only person with internet capability. If she figured this out, he would have a lot of explaining to do.

"Nah, just trying to get an email out to family. It's frustrating. I needed a new computer anyway."

"Okay," Cindy replied. Seeing the young man crush the computer seemed odd, but considering the circumstances, people may do all sorts of crazy things.

"What's going on over there?" Geonwon wanted to change the subject and hide if he could. He used the small crowd gathering around Joe's Jeep as a distraction.

"I don't know," Cindy replied.

At the same time, the real Incident Command was still reeling with the reality of the situation.

The CIA didn't have any idea who had committed this act and wanted none of the blame, while agent Petrov of the FBI was trying to put together a strategy to either stop the meltdown from occurring or at least apprehend the perpetrators afterward.

Joe Reece was setting up his Prussian Blue distribution center. The center consisted of his cases of the medicine setting in the bed of his Jeep. He recognized most of the people walking by. A woman about the same age as his daughter and a young Asian man came near. The woman approached and stopped, but the man kept walking.

"What are you doing?" Cindy asked the elderly man.

"Setting up a distribution center for Prussian Blue. If there's a release from the power plant, this stuff can block some of the radiation, maybe save some lives," Joe responded.

Geonwon overheard this and thought that this was a useless gesture and kept walking.

Cindy asked if she could help Joe, and he was about to reply yes, when she saw Hanna and Taylor.

"Hold on," she told Joe and then yelled, "Hanna!"

Hanna, Taylor, Troy, and Kara were walking along the road of stopped and abandoned cars when Hanna heard someone shout her name.

"*Cindy!*" Hanna almost shrieked.

Cindy ran to her old friend and the group of strangers she was walking with. They hugged each other tightly. They had missed each other but also sought comfort in the midst of the new realities they were facing. When they relaxed their embrace, Hanna introduced her to Troy and Kara.

Then Joe asked Taylor if he had figured out how to navigate with the watch yet.

"No, I haven't. Can you show me how?"

"I'm afraid we're out of sunlight, which we need to navigate by watch. I'll explain it to you, and we'll see if you can do it tomorrow." Joe paused long enough to take a pull from his lucky canteen and reach back into the cab. He pulled out a bag of beef jerky.

"Forget to bring a coat?" Joe asked.

Taylor was beginning to get cold.

Joe reached back into the cab and pulled out a small army top. It was huge on Taylor, but it was warm. Joe placed most of the beef jerky into one of the pockets and fed the rest to Beau.

Joe continued, "Hold your arm up flat. You point the hour hand at the sun. Now, it's important not to look directly at the sun. Picture an imaginary arrow halfway between the hour hand and the twelve o'clock position. This is south. When you face south, east is on your left, west is on your right, and north is at your back. This trick only works in the northern hemisphere, but that's where we are, so tomorrow, you're going to show us directions."

Joe didn't figure the young man would remember all this information overnight, but he was more concerned with giving him a task that would take his mind off all the excitement of this gypsy camp.

Taylor and Beau immediately liked Joe. Taylor liked the fact that Joe knew about all kinds of cool army stuff. Beau liked the fact that Joe was nice and had a seemingly endless supply of beef jerky.

Hanna, Cindy, Troy, and Kara continued talking, ignoring the bond that was forming between Joe, Taylor, and Beau.

Joe was now sitting on one of the cases of Prussian Blue. Taylor was sitting on another one a few feet away.

"Do you think this was caused by the Badgers?" Taylor asked.

"Badgers? I don't think Badgers had anything to do with this. Bad people caused this mess. The Red Hill Power Plant has been here for many years. Red Hill powers your television, computers, refrigerator, stoves, all that stuff. Bad people are trying to destroy it and let all the radiation out of the reactors. That's what this whole mess is about. I hope the police or the army or the Marines can stop it, but I don't know. That's why the stuff in these cases we're sitting on is so important. If there's a release, I'm going to make sure that you get the first dose of this stuff. It blocks radiation." Joe didn't want to explain any more to him. This was not an issue that children should have to worry about. He opened his canteen again and took another healthy slug.

"What's the coolest thing you've ever seen?" Taylor's new friend was cool. He had all kinds of army stuff and even drank from a canteen.

Joe struggled with that question. He had been all over the world as a young man in the military. He had seen his fair share of good and bad over the years. He didn't know what a kid of Taylor's age would consider cool.

"Taylor, I've been all over the world. I've seen a few cool things. Probably the coolest was this summer. I've seen the moon rising in Vietnam, Germany, and in many places in the U.S., but this summer was the Strawberry Moon. It was special this time because it happened at the same time as the summer solstice. It rose in the East and was a beautiful pink for about the first twenty minutes. You can see all sorts of things on the television or on a computer, but physically witnessing it for real in nature was cool. The last one was in June of 1967. I was in the army then and didn't get a chance to see it, but I witnessed this one."

"When is the next one?" Taylor asked.

"2062," Joe replied.

"Are you going to watch that one?"

Joe laughed. He laughed harder than he had laughed in a long time. Young Taylor didn't quite comprehend complicated issues such as mortality yet, and Joe didn't feel the need to burden him with it.

"You never can tell," Joe replied.

The innocence of the question also made Joe think about other things than himself and the sadness that had crept up on him recently. He started to think about this young man and his future. Joe didn't have much to offer to the world anymore, but he might be able to offer some sort of future to this young man.

An idea hit him, and he started to speak like one of the televangelists that he used to change the channel on. "Look, we can probably walk out of here! Wreck or no wreck, we can at least walk up to the interstate. They should be able to see that we're all Americans, some of us former military. Some of us too young to do something like this, and some of us too old. Either way, we should be able to get there, and if they see women and children, they may let us through!" A look of solemnity came over the group, as everyone looked at each other in a helpless fashion.

Joe wasn't done.

"You!" Joe shouted at Kara and Troy Felzer. "You could walk this young man and his mom right out of here. I'm too old. But just ten years ago, I would have put this boy on my shoulders if needed and walked him and his mom out of here!"

This probing from Joe just reaffirmed what Troy had been thinking. Even if the army turned back the adults, hopefully, they would at least take the kid.

"Agreed," Troy bellowed out. "Kara and I will walk him and his mom to the interstate. If the army lets them out, then great. If not, I guess we'll all meet back here."

Joe stepped forward, handed Troy a Ka-Bar knife, and said "Hopefully, you won't need this, but take it anyway. Good luck."

CHAPTER 28

Troy, Kara, Hanna, and Taylor started the slow walk to the interstate. They weaved between cars, but after some lewd proposals, mainly directed at Kara, they started walking on the shoulder of the road.

"Damn!" Kara said. "You would think in an apocalypse, people would have their minds on something else."

Hanna cringed at the thought, but maybe in an apocalypse, that might be a very common thought. The idea of young Troy as their protector was somewhat comforting, except that all he had was a knife. There had already been a few gunshots in the distance.

Luckily, they were only subject to a few more catcalls. Along the way, they met people who wanted to barter, mostly for batteries for emergency radios, but also for some other goods. Troy ended up trading the Ka-Bar knife for a bag of Doritos.

Hanna was angered. "Doritos won't do us much good if we get attacked!"

Troy pulled up his shirt to show her the .357 long barrel he had been keeping concealed.

"Oh." She wasn't as worried now.

The .357 might as well have been a water pistol. When they reached the interstate, not only were little green men waiting with a blockade, but an airplane was flying overhead with more little green men parachuting out of it.

An angry red-headed staff sergeant told them to return to their vehicles. The argument from Troy, Kara, and Hanna did nothing to change his mind.

They were all shocked that the U.S. Army was treating them as a potential enemy. Taylor wished that these army guys were nice, like Joe.

CHAPTER 29

At the on-ramp to the interstate, the army was clearing a path. The strategic national stockpile, which held medication and supplies for disasters, had arrived on a truck and was accepted by Captain Jennifer Lofton from the Army National Guard.

Captain Lofton knew that the road was in complete gridlock, and the chance of delivering medicine in a Humvee would be almost impossible. The only option was to send one platoon in to see who needed medicine or treatment. The chances of the local people—she refused to think of them as refugees—being hostile to the army was a possibility, so she authorized live ammo for the task.

She called Staff Sergeant Jacob Nash over to her vehicle. "I need your platoon to go in and see if any of the locals need medicine or medical treatment. It's not that cold out, so I'm not worried about anyone freezing to death. I have no idea why we're without internet or phone. That's above my pay grade, but I checked the weather before we got here. I want you to all go in locked and loaded. I doubt you'll be attacked, but we have to prepare for a scenario where the citizens turn against us," she ordered.

"Yes ma'am. I'll take third platoon, Williams, Smith, and Hong, with me."

"Good luck, Jacob," she finished.

Nash smiled. Even in the Guard, people rarely used first names, but Captain Lofton and Sergeant Nash had known each other for many years and through several deployments. They had seen their fair share of combat together.

Today was different. Jacob didn't believe that there would be any trouble from the civilian population. They would be scared, angry, and confused, but Jacob and his men didn't have any answers for them. They did have water, MREs, and medicine. Hopefully, they would see the army as the good guys, even though they had been ordered to block the interstate.

Geonwon had walked through the woods. When he had made it almost to the interstate, he paused. The army blockade was set up, and there were soldiers patrolling in groups. *Did they see him? No, hopefully not yet.*

He retreated into the woods and watched. He was out of food. He was out of water. He was out of familiar territory as well. His training in the North Korean Army had more to do with computers than actual soldiering. *Are there bears here? Snakes?*

He had planned on making it out of town before things got this bad. He suddenly felt the strong need to urinate. He didn't know if that was due to nerves or if it had just been a long time since he had gone. He looked over his right and then his left shoulder as he urinated in the woods. He then sat down behind some of the thicker brush and watched the roadblock.

At dusk, he watched as four men from the army started walking away from the blockade and into the gridlocked cars. Geonwon stayed in the tree line but followed the men. They were handing out medical supplies and water.

As he got closer, he was relieved that one of the men was of Asian descent. This was the one he followed as the men started to split up.

Private First Class Hong handed out his last MRE. He was hungry himself. Luckily, it was almost time to make his way back to the blockade and grab some more. So far, people had a lot of questions for him, for which he had no answers.

A young nervous-looking man sitting on the edge of the tree line called out to him. As Hong approached him, the young man coughed and stood up.

"Are you okay?" Hong asked.

The young man started backing away into the woods.

"Hey, are you all right?" Hong repeated.

The young man stopped a few feet into the woods and crouched down.

As Hong approached, the man looked up and asked him if he had any asthma inhalers.

Hong looked inside the bag of medical supplies that he was carrying. "I don't think I do, but…"

Hong didn't get to finish his sentence. Geonwon had

grabbed a large rock, and when Hong turned his attention to the contents of the supply bag, Geonwon caved in his skull. He was careful not to let any of the blood from the soldier run down onto the uniform.

As Geonwon went about stealing the uniform from the dead soldier, his mind began to process the probability that civilians would leave him alone if he were dressed as a soldier. The fact that this guy had been named Hong was even luckier for Geonwon.

But he had to be careful to avoid other soldiers. They would obviously know that he was not one of their comrades.

This soldier had been carrying a loaded M16A2 rifle. Geonwon thought about this as well. If he had to shoot his way out, his chances for escape would be almost nonexistent. He almost left the rifle, but then thought it might be odd to see an unarmed soldier, so he picked it up.

It was getting dark. He formulated a quick plan in his head: He could walk past most of the cars toward the army roadblock and then head off into the woods before reaching the roadblock. With any luck, he wouldn't run into any of the other soldiers. If he made it that far, he could bypass the roadblock through the woods and hopefully hitchhike his way out of here.

Geonwon's position in the army dictated that he spend all of his time in front of a computer. In the woods, in the dark, he was out of his element. The M16 he carried in his hands was the ultimate double-edged sword. He could shoot it in an extreme emergency, but that would attract what looked like a whole division of people who would be happy to put a bullet in him, or at least ensure him an expedited ride to Guantanamo Bay. *Mission over! Family dead! He could not allow thoughts like these to cloud his head! He had created a masterpiece of a program, defeated the American capitalists! Now the only thing standing between him and his family was a small wooded area and some Yankee soldiers. He would prevail!*

The United States Army had not established a command post at the interstate. They were setting one up as Geonwon walked slightly to the south of it. He continued to walk. The boots he stole from Private Hong were two sizes larger than what Geonwon wore. Blisters started to form on his feet, warm and thick. *How much more walking could he do? Would anyone suspect him of deserting the army this close to where they were set up?*

Geonwon decided that he had made it far enough from the exit to try his hand at hitchhiking. He was several miles away from the exit that blocked Red Hill from the rest of the nation. He believed that the army uniform would help.

He tossed his rifle in the ditch as he walked out of the woods and up to the interstate. He nervously looked at his watch. Not making it to the rendezvous point to collect his money was not an option. He was supposed to meet his contact in Florida. Geonwon would supply the bank account and routing number for the funds to the contact, who would then deposit that money into the account. If Geonwon didn't make it by November 3, the contact would assume he had been caught or killed and move on.

Geonwon's head was swimming in confusion. *Could he make it to Florida in time by hitchhiking? If not, should he steal another car? Or should he just kill the first person who stopped and take their car? It would be the fastest way, if he didn't get caught. Why was the rendezvous site so far away?*

RED HILL

Geonwon had only killed one person in his life. He had killed a soldier named Hong. He knew that his operation to destroy the nuclear facility would likely kill many people. But he did that with a computer. Killing Hong had been different. The two had been face to face, and Hong thought that he was there to help. This gave Geonwon an uneasy feeling in his stomach. Could he do it again if he had to? He didn't know.

After killing Hong, Geonwon had gone through the contents of his wallet. There was an ID, a twenty-dollar bill, and a debit card. Geonwon pocketed these items.

He had gone to put the soldier's hat on his head when he noticed something on the inside of the hat. It was a picture of a young woman and child tucked into the lining. Geonwon placed the hat on his head and continued. There was no time to feel guilty.

A Honda Odyssey pulled over on the right side of the highway. Geonwon sped up to a slow jog, glad that he was making some progress as the blisters on his feet begged him to slow down.

The back glass of the minivan looked like a billboard for the occupants of the van. It had stickers declaring the sports that the children participated in, and on the left side of the glass near the bottom, there was a sticker for each member of the family. This made him feel uneasy. He didn't want to kill anyone else, let alone a family of people. The thought of killing children almost made him vomit again, but he didn't. Instead, he put a large smile on his face as the side of the van opened.

"Hello, young soldier!" the driver of the van said.

"Hello," Geonwon replied in his most American accent.

"Where are you heading?" the driver asked.

Geonwon thought about this. He didn't want anyone to know that he was heading to Florida. As a soldier in the North Korean Army, he had extensively studied the United States military. He knew enough to sound convincing.

"Fort Benning, Georgia," Geonwon replied.

The man turned from the driver's seat and shook his hand. "My name's Ryan Hilbert. This is my son Steven. You're a long way from Fort Benning. Are you apart of the craziness that's happening in Red Hill?"

"I was visiting some friends on leave. I was told to report back to base. My car broke down, so I figured I would hitchhike," Geonwon replied.

"Why not take a bus?'" Ryan asked.

"I don't want to spend the money," Geonwon replied.

"Okay. We're going as far as Evansville; you're welcome to ride with us. After that, you'll have to find another ride. What do you do in the army?" Ryan asked.

Geonwon thought about this for a second. He didn't want to have a long conversation. He knew that the more things he said, the more likely this man was to decide that he was lying. *What job could I pick that would seem boring and make these people not want to talk?*

"I'm a cook. I plan on using the GI bill for college," Geonwon answered.

"Good idea. It's a safe job, and you still get the benefits. Plus, you can always work at a restaurant if needed when finishing off school. Very smart. What do you want to study in school?" Ryan asked.

"History," Geonwon replied.

"History. Well, there are not a lot of jobs for history majors. Have you considered engineering?" Ryan asked.

"Possibly," Geonwon replied.

"I'm a software engineer. It's good work. You might want to consider it. Beats sweating in a hot kitchen," Ryan replied.

The excitement of the last few days had caught up with Geonwon. He leaned his head back and was asleep in seconds. He began to dream. He dreamt of the woman whose car he stole the license plate from. He followed her into the woods. She started to run, and he ran after her until he could no longer keep up. As he slowed to a fast walk, he thought he heard her. He followed her voice through an area of dense brush. On the other side of the brush was his family. His father looked at him in disgust. "You are no better than the murderers that put us in camps!"

His father pointed off in the distance. There was a person in a hazmat suit. Geonwon approached the figure. He was winded from the run and was bent slightly at the waist, trying to catch his breath. He was looking at the boots of the suit.

As he straightened his body, his gaze went from the rubber boots up to the plastic bag that comprised most of the suit. When Geonwon looked in the facepiece of the suit, he thought it looked like a space suit, and he knew at once who the suit belonged to. It was Private Hong. Part of Hong's skull was missing, and Geonwon could see drying tissues in the early stages of decay.

Geonwon screamed and ran past Hong and ended up in the seat of the van he was now riding in. Only this time, the girl he followed into the woods was sitting beside him. She handed him the rock that he had used to kill private Hong. Hong's blood was still on the rock, dried and flaky.

He put the rock close to his face and smelled a faint coppery odor. He paused as he considered killing the driver of the van and his son. He looked back to the right, and the lady nodded as though she knew what he was thinking.

He promptly smashed Ryan and then Steven over the head. Then his body locked up in terror as he thought about the car veering off the road after the driver was killed. He expected it to lurch off the highway immediately. But the van kept going in a straight line down the road.

Geonwon looked to his right. The girl was no longer there. He looked down at his hands. The rock was also gone.

He looked up to see Ryan and Steven. Their bodies still faced forward, but their skulls were turned at an impossible angle, facing Geonwon.

Steven spoke first. "We knew that you weren't an American soldier. You are the terrorist who was sent here to destroy the power plant. You are foolish."

Then Ryan spoke, grinning as blood and saliva ran down his chin. "Your programming is poor. Do you really think that you can cause a meltdown? You'll fail. Failure equals death in your business, doesn't it? Where did you learn to code, in some third-world country? I bet it was the Ahobiryong Mountains. What do you think will happen when you fail? Will the Lebanese hit you over the head with a rock? No, I'm sure they have other plans for you. Your father is dying as we speak in a labor camp. He's starving because the moral terrorist who is blowing up a power plant was too high and mighty to fudge a few expense reports. His last breath is running out of his lungs now. You were right. They are in Russia. As he lies dying at this very moment, he's ashamed of you. So is your mother. What did she always tell you? She told you that you are smart but forgetful. Tell me Geonwon, did you remember to put fuel in the second generator? Without it, your plan fails. Even if your amateur programming were to succeed, the computer must have electricity to execute the commands.

"It will work!" Geonwon exclaimed, waking up and startling the other occupants of the van.

"Bad dream?" asked Steven.

Geonwon was sweating profusely. "I suppose," he replied. But it wasn't a bad dream; tt was a mind-shattering nightmare.

Geonwon started going over the plan that he had meticulously crafted and rehearsed repeatedly. *Was there enough fuel in the generators to keep the computers running? The generators were supposed to be the quietest on the market, but what if someone heard them?*

This was bullshit, he decided. Nothing more than a bad dream.

He then remembered the conversation he had with himself at the doughnut shop. This was just his mind making him feel guilty. He would continue to the rendezvous point, meet his contact, get his money, and then try to locate his family.

Geonwon looked out the window to see a sign that read "EVANSVILLE 10 MILES." Stealing another car was a huge risk. He also didn't want to kill the two people who generously picked him up on the side of the interstate.

The propaganda produced in his homeland was bullshit. Americans didn't want to annihilate his country. According to a

YouTube video he watched, many Americans couldn't even find the DPRK on a map.

He knew that he was about to kill many good people just like this. It made his mood plunge into an irritated and depressed state. It was nice here. Smuggling his family to a country like this would be his goal if he could rescue them. But that would have to come later.

CHAPTER 30

OCTOBER 29

The sun was just beginning to rise on what looked like an automotive graveyard. Cindy Peller hadn't slept well at all. This was the first time since college that she had slept in her car, and the pain in her lower back was a clear reminder of why.

In the car next to her were Troy and Kara, both of whom she had met the previous night. A few cars in front of them slept Hanna and Taylor. They had sat around a fire like a bunch of campers till late in the evening, and now she could smell the woodsmoke that had permeated her clothes.

Cindy was cold and hoped that the fire was still going. Closing her door with the handle pulled up, trying not to wake the others, she walked to the campfire.

Instead of a dwindled-down fire, it was as large as it had

been the last night. Joe was sitting fireside with some sort of metal container hanging over the fire.

"Good morning," said Joe.

"Good morning," Cindy replied.

"Would you like a cup of coffee?" he asked.

"I could kill for a cup! Where is it?"

"In the canteen cup." Joe pointed to the cup he had hanging over the fire. "It's instant, but any port in a storm, right?"

This made Cindy grin. "I suppose so."

"Good morning, everyone. I still can't reach anyone on the CB." Troy appeared and sat near the fire as well.

"I would assume the government's using some sort of signal jammer to keep terrorists from being able to communicate as well as keeping citizens from organizing," Joe said. As ominous as the words were, Joe had a satisfied look on his face. He was only a few minutes away from the coffee he had taken out of the MREs.

Hanna and Taylor now joined the group.

"Would you like a hot dog?" Joe asked Taylor. "Maybe not the best breakfast, but you could use something. I have some MRE hot dogs. I know that the MRE has a heater in it, but I think they're much better over a fire. Have you ever roasted a hot dog?"

"No," Taylor said spiritedly.

Hanna thought to herself that surely he had, but she couldn't think of a time when he might have. She welcomed the activity since Taylor could be fidgety in the morning. This would give him something to do.

Joe took the ancient Ka-Bar knife out of a leather sheath on his belt and began to sharpen a green limb from a small tree.

"You start with a green limb. If you use a dead branch, it can catch fire and ruin the hot dog. You then carve the bark from the limb." Joe did this in slow, careful strokes.

"Another important thing is to roast slowly over the coals at the base of the fire. If you roast at the top where the flames are, you burn the outside, and the inside will still be cold."

Neither Joe nor Hanna knew if he was processing all of this, but he seemed content.

Taylor looked back at his mom. "Maybe I can get a knife like that for Christmas."

The look on Hanna's face was not a hopeful one.

"This is a knife for a professional soldier or a Marine. You are way too young for a knife like this. But I was looking through my stuff this morning, and I think I found just what you need," Joe said with a grin.

He reached into his jacket pocket and told Taylor to hold out his hand and close his eyes. Taylor did, and when he opened them again, he was holding a red-handled pocket knife with a cross on the side.

"This is a Swiss Army Knife. People have carried these for generations. It has two blades, a pair of scissors, a file, a corkscrew, and a saw. Everything a young man needs to get into and out of trouble." Joe smiled at Hanna.

She returned the smile and didn't know whether she should be happy or worried. "What do you say?" she asked Taylor.

"Thank you," Taylor replied.

"No problem. But remember to always cut away from you. We can work with it later," Joe said.

"Always good advice," said Frank Coleman.

The crowd turned to meet Frank and Janice. They introduced themselves to the group and split the last of the coffee from the canteen cup.

Frank and Joe had known each other for years. Frank had been a scout leader when his kids were younger and often turned to Joe for interesting outdoor ideas when he was running low.

"Have you shown him the watch navigation trick yet?" Frank asked.

"We're working on that one today," Joe replied.

"What about the two-stick method?" Frank asked.

"I was saving that one for later. If we're here for a while, I'll show him how to make fire and water purification," Joe replied with a smile.

Taylor ran over to a clearing to practice his new watch trick. Beau ran along with Taylor, always ready, although he didn't run as fast as he used to. Hanna was thinking about how long Beau might live with his slowing pace showing his years. Taylor was young and hadn't noticed his sidekick slowing down.

Joe looked the group around the fire. "Okay, now that the boy's out of earshot, how much does anyone really know about this situation? I have the Prussian Blue, but does anyone know what we should be looking for? I assume a mushroom cloud or a blast of some sort, right?"

Frank was eager to respond with almost textbook precision, reciting the things he had learned working as a fireman.

"There won't be a mushroom cloud, even if there is a meltdown. It's a reactor, not a bomb. It's a different design than

Chernobyl. When I was with the fire department, we trained for issues with the plant. Basically, if everything goes to shit and they can't keep the reactor at a certain temperature, they do what is called a SCRAM. That's where they put all the control rods into the reactor, forcing it to shut down."

Cindy asked, "It doesn't sound like they can do that. If they could, wouldn't all of this be over?"

"I suppose so, but even if they can't do that, the reactor will just overpressurize," Frank responded.

"Then what would happen?" Hanna asked.

"Well, that's still bad. It means that radiation will be released. It will eventually dissipate somewhat, but the town and the surrounding area would be uninhabitable for several hundred years. The wind direction will create a plume, carrying radiation in a concentrated area until it dissipates." Frank was trying to help, but this news was only slightly better than a mushroom cloud.

Just as Frank was finishing his explanation, Kara noticed another person walking toward the group.

Yelena Harris, a late riser, had been dreaming of the trip she took to the St. Louis Zoo in the fifth grade. There were giraffes, elephants, bears, and of course, cotton candy. She was home arguing with her brother over whether you could see the arch from the zoo. He always wore camouflage, even though he wouldn't be joining the Marines for another ten years.

"You can't see it from there!" Steven exclaimed.

"Yes, you can!" Yelena shouted back.

"It doesn't matter now," her dad said. "It's all gone now. The reactor at Red Hill blew up." He turned on the television to show all the animals blackened like a marshmallow over a stove.

Yelena suddenly woke. She didn't know how long she had been out, but Tank was snoring in the front seat. Bill appeared to be sleeping as well but without the snoring. She needed to go to the restroom but didn't see one anywhere. She opened the rear passenger side door and slid out, careful not to wake her newfound travel companions.

She closed the door as quietly as she could, easing the handle down. Bill stirred but then went back to sleep.

They were still in a traffic jam, but many of the cars were empty. She could see a small group in the distance, but no bathroom. She hadn't used the bathroom outside since she was a child and wasn't looking forward to it today. Thankfully, a number one, she thought; no toilet paper to be seen. She walked deeper into the woods and completed her task when the faint sound of footsteps started to close in.

She turned around to see Bill.

"Just checking on you. Never know what type of people are camping out here waiting for some type of doomsday shit," he said.

"Thanks." Yelena wasn't scared, but she had an odd feeling. She couldn't quite place it, but she somehow felt uneasy in the woods, though safer with Bill around.

"Like I said, we don't know who's out here. I spotted a group up ahead. There's a kid and a golden retriever with them, so I'm going to assume they're harmless, but just in case they aren't, I think we should walk through the woods and check them out first."

"And if they're a bunch of cannibal, rapist ninjas?" she jokingly asked.

Bill pulled up the right pant leg above his boot to expose a 9-millimeter Glock pistol.

Yelena frowned. She hated guns but knew that in a worst-case scenario, they may need one to survive.

They started walking through the woods.

"We're going to sweep wide and approach as quietly as we can," Bill muttered.

"I've seen the movie *Predator* if that helps," she said with a smile.

Bill couldn't help but to let out a chuckle. "That'll help."

As they got closer to the group, Bill grabbed her hand. She didn't know if he was just being chivalrous or if he was just a very shy romantic.

Bill's heart was racing. He was somewhat apprehensive about groups of people in a crisis, and at the same time, infatuated with the woman who had given them a ride.

CHAPTER 31

Tank awoke to a very sore neck and an even sorer disposition. Bill was gone. So was Yelena. He didn't know if they just went for a walk or if something had happened to them, although that didn't seem likely.

He had noticed Bill looking in the rearview mirror often to check on Yelena. Tank sensed that his buddy Bill may be a little more than thankful to the woman for giving them a lift. He could understand in a way. She seemed very familiar, almost like they had met somewhere before. *Maybe in high school?* But that wasn't likely it. *Could she have been a dancer from Diamond Dolls earlier in life?* Maybe, but that was an issue he would figure out later. For now, his plan was to talk to the people around the campfire to see if anyone had seen them.

As Tank approached the group, an older man was explaining something to them about a meltdown. An even older man in camouflage was standing by the cases of Prussian

Blue that Tank remembered from the storeroom at Bull Creek Military Surplus.

Tank took off his overshirt, revealing the MMA tank top he had been wearing underneath. He was hoping to appear intimidating and menacing.

Before anyone spoke to him, he started the conversation. "How much would you take for one of those cases of Prussian Blue?" Tank stood ramrod straight, trying to appear taller than his five-foot-nine frame, but Joe wasn't concerned with him in the least.

"It's not for sale. If it's needed, I'll give it to the women and children first. Then we can draw straws or some other horseshit for the remaining doses." While he was saying this, he realized how much of a liability having all that Prussian Blue out in the open could make him in the wake of a meltdown.

"I think that you may all be overestimating the effectiveness of the medicine," Frank chimed in. "In the event of a meltdown, that medicine will keep some of the radiation from being absorbed by your thyroid, but if we're in the path of the plume, or even just too close to the plant when it happens, you can swallow every Persian Blue pill we have out here, and it won't do a bit of good. The beta and gamma radiation will kill us all. Or make us wish we were dead. The only thing those pills can do is give us a slightly better chance if we're far enough away in the first place. Truthfully, I don't think we are. I also think the army's keeping us from leaving, hoping that the terrorist is among us and not crazy enough to cause the meltdown before escaping. It's obvious that they should have been able to move the wrecked vehicle out of the way by now. Besides, anyone with a 4x4 could bypass it on the median. There's a lot more going on here than we know, and I think we owe it to ourselves to figure that out. We can stay here and draw straws for pills that'll do little good, or we can go out to the interstate and try to find out what is happening."

"We already tried that," Troy said.

Kara chimed in. "I think you're right. The army acted like we came straight out of Kabul."

Frank continued to talk about strategy and the effect of Prussian Blue. When he finished, he looked at the rest of the group. He was hoping that what he said would ease some of the tension of the townspeople who had now become refugees in their own land. The thought of people fighting each other over a useless medicine deeply upset him. In retrospect, the talk didn't do much good.

Janice, who up till now had been silent, joined the conversation.

"I don't know how much good that stuff will do, but I'm old, and I've had my time. I want to make sure that my share goes to that little boy and his mom."

"That's really touching, Granny," Tank sarcastically replied.

Joe was both touched by the selflessness of the elderly woman and angered at Tank's rudeness to someone who was so old and kind. "Your dumb ass isn't going to get one single pill!" Joe yelled at Tank. "You're what's wrong with this country in the first place! You're wearing camouflage pants and a tank top. But I bet you haven't spent five minutes in the military! As a matter of fact, I'm sure of it. That shirt has glitter on it like a schoolgirl would wear. What does MMA even stand for? Men's Makeup and

Accessories? You're a posing chicken hawk! I bet you're one of those people who want us to go to war all over the globe, but I bet you don't have a DD 214. You and that other idiot, who I'm sure is running around here somewhere, probably off posing in the woods in his camo pants, think that you should get the medicine first. Well, you won't."

Frank was worried that the younger man might attack Joe at any second and stepped between them.

Tim Baylor, the presumptive governor-elect, and George Mendoza were approaching the group. Deputies Ford and Kepler werde still asleep in the police Blazer.

Bill and Yelena, hearing the argument between Tank and the old man, started running through the woods toward the group.

Tank reached behind his back and pulled out a snub-nose .38 from a waistband holster. He pointed it at Joe's head and commanded,

"You're going to give me a case of pills, or you're going to die out here at the side of this road!"

Tim Baylor drew his service pistol and sprinted toward the group. He screamed, "Police! Drop your weapons!"

Bill and Yelena had now entered the clearing from the woods with the 9-millimeter Glock drawn.

A screaming match ensued between Tank, Bill, Tim Baylor, Yelena, and Hanna. Tank threatened to kill Joe in front of Taylor.

Tim Baylor yelled, "Drop the gun, or I'll put two in the back of your head."

Carl wondered to himself if any of these people knew how satisfying it was to kill another human being. He further considered how much less fun it would be with a gun.

Bill realized that Tank had brought this on himself and placed his gun on the ground, hoping that the sheriff and the sleepy-looking deputies Ford and Kepler, who had just arrived at the clearing, would not shoot him and Yelena if a gunfight broke out.

Yelena thought the whole scene looked like the ending to the movie *Reservoir Dogs* when the criminals all shot each other in a circle.

Beau had decided that he had had enough of the screaming. Fearing the possibility of harm coming to Taylor or Hanna, he decided to sink his teeth into Tank's leg right above the knee.

Tank screamed and writhed in pain. Before he could turn the gun on the dog, Frank and Baylor wrestled the gun out of his hand.

Tank punched Beau on the top of his head, which caused him to loosen and then release the bite, but the damage had been done. Tank's leg was spraying blood, and he fell to the ground. He meant to ramble off another threat about what he was going to do to that dog, but instead, he passed out.

Frank started to treat the wound with one of Joe's first-aid kits. Deputy Kepler started to handcuff Tank, figuring that it would be much easier to do while Tank was passed out.

Tim Baylor told him not to. "Just take his gun. We don't even have a place to lock him up for now."

"We'll be taking all of the guns," a voice called out from seemingly nowhere.

The group turned away from Tank to see that they were surrounded by soldiers.

"I don't think so! This is still America!" Bill called out.

Sergeant Nash stepped forward and looked around at the group. "Sometime yesterday, when we were out here delivering food and medicine to all of you good citizens, someone murdered Private First Class Jason Hong. I don't know if it was anyone in this group, and I may never find out. But we're going to search every one of you and your vehicles and confiscate all your weapons. If you don't like it, you can sue me later, but rest assured, I am not going to lose another American soldier on American soil."

"You don't have that authority," Baylor responded.

"I have an M16 and so does everyone in my platoon. About a mile up the road is the rest of the company. They're all locked and loaded as well. They want revenge. Captain Lofton and myself are the only ones stopping them from coming down here and beating the truth out of one or all of you. Before you go on again about authority, you must realize that the United States Army is in charge of this area for the time being."

"Then tell us why in the hell we can't leave and why you guys are jamming phone and radio frequencies?" Frank yelled.

"That is above my pay grade. Besides, while you guys are whining about not being able to use phones and radios, one of my men was murdered!"

A female soldier walked out of the woods and stood beside Nash. She looked around at the group, noticing the apprehension as the civilians realized that the army was now in charge of a situation that was rapidly getting worse. She knew that her National Guard unit could overtake the civilians if needed. But at what cost? She could guarantee herself a court martial, a dishonorable discharge, and many years in prison, at the very least.

Besides, Captain Lofton wasn't as sure as Sargent Nash that any of these people had murdered Hong. Private Hong's uniform was missing as well as his rifle. The only good reason to do that would be to try to sneak by their roadblock.

Hong had been dead for hours when his body had been found. If whoever killed him did so to sneak by the army, then odds were that they had been successful and were possibly long gone. There wasn't anything she could do about this, but she was determined not to let this situation turn into a bloodbath.

She decided to address the group. "My name is Captain Jennifer Lofton. I am in command of the Army National Guard unit that has sealed off the highway. We have been ordered to stop anyone from leaving town or entering from the highway. It has been determined by the Department of Homeland Security that to keep the possibility of terrorists from communicating with each other or remotely detonating any bombs at chokepoints, such as this one, all cell service and radio communication will be disabled. That's the reason that none of your phones or citizen band radios work.

"We've only been here about fifteen hours, and we've heard all sorts of rumors concerning FEMA camps and other crazy conspiracy theories. I want you all to know that there is no government plot against you. We are not federal troops, even though we have been activated. All the soldiers that you see here in these woods are local people from within about fifty miles of here. This is our community too. We do not want to see a meltdown any more than you do.

"There's a very real terrorist threat against this area. That's due to some person or organization trying to cause a meltdown at the power plant. Currently, some of the best minds in the country are working on a solution. I'm certain that one will be found before a meltdown occurs.

"One of our men was murdered out here, and when this is over, we will turn back command of the area to civilian law enforcement. While we currently oversee law enforcement of the area, we lack the expertise to conduct these sorts of criminal investigations. We obviously don't have a CSI lab packed into a duffle bag out here in the woods. We have enough food and water to sustain everyone here for a few days.

"You're not being officially detained, although we can't let you enter the highway. Also, it would be foolish to go back toward the town since you would be moving closer to the power plant, which would put you at even more danger if the meltdown occurs.

"There's a possibility that one or more of you is a murderer, so I suggest that you go everywhere, even to use the restroom, in groups to lower the possibility of being attacked. We'll let you know more when we know more.

"I have a question for the group. Is there anyone here named George Mendoza?"

"Here." George raised his right hand.

"Good. We were given orders to deliver you to the power plant if we found you."

George walked over to Captain Lofton and Sergeant Nash. They shook hands and began to walk toward the interstate accompanied by four armed soldiers.

Sergeant Nash addressed his soldiers and the civilians in the automotive camp. "We're going to search all vehicles. I want every set of keys in a pile in front of me in the next five minutes.

After the car searches, we'll search individuals. The women will have to be patient because we only have two female soldiers to search you. Men will be searched by men, women by women until searches are complete. Fall out!"

"I'm fine with both of those women searching me," Tank called out.

The soldiers ignored Tank and started following the orders. Sergeant Nash and his platoon spread out, and within an hour, disarmed the entire population. He thought of it as a refugee camp but knew better than to say so out loud. He had instructed his soldiers not to use that term as well.

The search turned up fourteen rifles, fifty-three handguns, and various knives, but no trace of Private Hong's M16. The only army uniforms found in the search were the ones that the old man with the surplus store had. They were woodland camouflage, the type of uniform that had been used from the early 1980s until about 2004. They obviously had not been Hong's uniform.

None of the civilians put up any resistance, but the old man with the surplus gear did have something to say to Sergeant Nash as he was being searched. "I earned my stripes in Nam. What about you?"

"Iraq," Nash replied.

The searching continued in almost complete silence. American civilian soldiers searching American civilians in hometown USA. The National Guardsmen, some who had searched enemy combatants in lands far away, now performed similar searches on people who delivered their mail, or in the case of Corporal Stephens, the man who delivered his child Phillip.

"Sorry, Dr. Pearson, I have to do this," Stephens apologized.

"I understand." Dr. William Pearson reluctantly handed over a nickel-plated .357. "I expect to get that back when this all blows over."

"I'll supply a hand receipt, Doctor. And I'll make sure you get it back," Stephens replied.

"How's Phillip?" Dr. Pearson asked.

"His mom took him to her parents' house in Ohio as soon as this started. They were lucky to get out in time."

"They were lucky," Pearson agreed and nodded.

After confiscating all the weapons and issuing hand receipts to the reluctant owners, the soldiers left three cases of MREs for the evening's dinner.

"That's all the shit you've got for us?" Bill growled. "Can't you guys make a McDonald's run or something?"

"We're the National Guard, not Haliburton. We're eating MREs for dinner tonight as well," Sergeant Nash responded.

Bill stepped up and opened the first case of MREs. "Well, at least the tortellini's not too bad." He handed the packaged meal to Yelena.

"Are there some survival red wine rations in there as well?" Yelena asked with a smirk.

"I'll check, but I think that the navy are the only ones who get wine. Even if we did, I don't have a corkscrew." Bill was grinning as he said this.

"I have one!" Taylor stepped forward with his new Swiss Army Knife.

Bill was now laughing as he told Taylor that it wouldn't be needed.

Carl Rothscoat would have also liked some red wine. He was sitting under a large sycamore tree pondering the day's events. Someone else had been murdered. This helped draw attention away from him.

He was at least partially sure that George Mendoza suspected him of the murder of Irwin Poole. That didn't matter as much to him as his belief that Sheriff Tim Baylor likely suspected him of it too. Deputies Ford and Kepler probably didn't suspect much of anything. They seemed like very simple-minded people, the same type of people who would have elected him as governor. This made him happy, but the new problem for Carl was that he wanted to do it again.

He scanned the crowd. The muscle-bound man who wanted to beat him up a day before could now only limp from place to place due to a dog bite. Carl would like to lure him away from the crowd and maybe run a sharp branch into his heart. But that would be too much like the first time. If he could buy some time alone, maybe he could think of something more inventive.

Beau was good (as dogs tend to be) at determining kind people from cruel people. Joe was kind. The man who almost attacked him was not, so he bit him to protect Joe. But there was someone worse than him in the crowd. Across the road, a man sat under a large tree. Beau only knew a few things about humans, but he knew that this one was the worst he had ever come across.

Beau didn't turn his back on him as everyone started eating food out of bags. Taylor and Hanna would likely feed him from one of them. He loved eating with his family much more than he liked to eat alone. But this food didn't smell nearly as good as the pizza he had had earlier in this trip.

With the promise of food, he could hopefully get the blood taste out of his mouth. Still, he would keep a wary eye out for the man under the tree.

CHAPTER 32

OCTOBER 30

Shawn and Dave had camped out the night before only a few hundred yards from the rest of the group. They ate the last few doughnuts around lunchtime and finished off the last of the beer a little after three in the afternoon.

"I think you must have thrown some poison ivy in the fire," Shawn said, scratching his forearm.

"What makes you say that?" Dave was now scratching his left shin right above the boot line.

"Because you gathered the wood for the fire." Shawn was uncomfortable, but not angry. In the previous three times when he had gotten poison ivy, he'd had to get a shot at the doctor's office. He knew that there was a slim chance of getting a shot for poison ivy out here in the woods. But he remained hopeful.

"Maybe the army or whoever stopped the meltdown," Shawn hoped out loud, changing the subject.

"What makes you think that?" Dave asked.

"Well, I haven't seen any mushroom clouds. Have you? I haven't heard any big explosions."

"No," Dave replied, "but what about an EMP? It's a pulse let out by a nuclear blast that kills all electronics."

"Well, we don't have cell signal, which is odd. Will the four-wheeler start? It's an electric start."

Dave pushed the button on the left handlebar. The Kawasaki sputtered and started.

"Okay, at least the four-wheeler will start. Let's park it in the woods, and I'll pull the spark plug. That way, if anyone finds it and tries to steal it, they'll be shit out of luck. I think we should walk to that group of cars up there and check it out."

"Okay," Dave said, scratching his shin as he threw his leg over the bike. "Maybe those people will have some calamine lotion."

After a few more minutes of scratching and trying to remember how EMPs work, they began to walk over to the group to see if anyone closer to the interstate had any information on what was happening.

Shawn and Dave didn't try to sneak up on the group; they didn't feel the need to. They figured they were likely to know most of the people. Besides, they had handed out free doughnuts to the drivers and passengers in those parked cars the day before.

Beau noticed the two guys first. He heard them, and then he smelled them and was reminded of the treats that Hanna and Taylor sometimes ate for breakfast. On good mornings, Taylor would drop some of the treats on the floor, which put them firmly in Beau's territory.

Kara noticed them next. She nudged Troy gently, who looked up.

"Do you know those guys?" she asked.

"I think they run the doughnut shop," he replied.

CHAPTER 33

Night was beginning to fall on the mass of cars and the group of stranded motorists. Joe and Taylor had foraged for wood most of the afternoon.

Taylor had learned to use the saw on his Swiss Army Knife to cut smaller, dryer branches and couldn't wait to cut a green limb to make his own hot dog stick for dinner this evening.

Beau went with them on their excursion, happy to be with Taylor and Joe, out in nature, free of the backyard fence.

Yelena Harris attended to Tank's dog bite. She told him that the likelihood of getting rabies from the dog was low. Her first-aid kit was slightly better than the military one that Joe reluctantly supplied. It was lacking some of the items from the hospital that she would have liked to have, but she patched up Tank and smiled to herself as she again remembered the bulletproof vest test. These men weren't the brightest, but she was starting to feel something for Bill Reilly. He was odd, but nice. There was no hope for Tank, she thought. He was apt to be on the losing end of life and might not live too long with his volatile temper.

Hanna Green and Cindy Peller were catching up on old times. It would have been nicer to do so with some Starbucks or maybe a glass of wine, but the two old friends were laughing and having a good time despite the circumstances.

Kara and Troy Felzer were becoming friends with Dave and Shawn. Dave had walked back to get the four-wheeler, and Kara was riding on the back of it with him. They all thought that fuel might be in short supply, but boredom had begun to set in. Kara treated the poison ivy on Dave and Shawn with some calamine lotion and cotton swabs from Yelena Harris.

Carl Rothscoat had left his spot under the sycamore tree and was now sitting in the woods, decompressing from the events of the last day. He watched the four-wheeler go through the woods.

Killing one of those people might bring him another high like the one he experienced when killing Irwin Poole. But the chances of getting caught were high. He would have to wait.

One of the soldiers blocking the interstate had been killed. Carl was jealous that he didn't get to do it. He started to think about who it could have been. Everyone in the group seemed very normal, like sheep. He was a wolf and didn't believe that any of them were.

Tank and Bill were a couple of deadheads. They seemed like the most likely, but they didn't have it in them. They were all about show, but they couldn't kill anyone. Talking tough is one thing he knew a lot about from the campaign trail. But to feel the last breath of a man as you drained it out of him was something neither of those wannabe tough guys would ever experience. He continued to ponder this as a few drops of rain hit his face.

Joe frowned upon the arrival of rain. It would be difficult to keep the fire going, if even possible. The wood that he and Taylor had stacked would get wet and be difficult to burn after the rain passed.

It was also getting cold. The fuel in his Jeep was below a half-tank. He didn't know how long they would all be there, but running out of fuel and wet firewood could make for a cold evening. He had a couple of cold-weather sleeping bags with waterproof covers. He would make sure that Taylor slept in one of these. He would also supply one to Janice Harmon. The whole situation was bad, but the thought of such an elderly person out here in this weather worried him.

Janice was less worried than anyone else in the crowd. She had lived a long and full life and wasn't too worried about how the rest of it would fall into place. She was more concerned about her kids and grandkids. She didn't know if they had made it out of town before it was blocked off. She had forgotten her phone with all their numbers preprogrammed in it at her house. The people who had phones had said that they weren't working anyway.

Sheriff Tim Baylor, Frank Coleman, and Deputies Ford and Kepler were discussing the legalities of the National Guard taking weapons from them.

"The only way they can legally take our weapons is if they're needed in an investigation. If the soldier hadn't been killed, then they couldn't have legally taken them. That's from the Stafford Act," Frank Coleman told the group.

"Screw the guns; they should have at least left us a tent," replied Deputy Ford.

"Or some more food," Kepler chimed in.

"I think we should be more concerned that there has been a murder in our town, two of them now, and there isn't a damn thing we can do about it," Sheriff Baylor inserted.

"Or the possibility that we may all die a horrific death," Frank Coleman reminded them.

The group stared at him.

"Well, it is a possibility," Frank said while shrugging his shoulders.

Bill Reilly and Yelena Harris were starting to become close. She enjoyed talking with him, and he liked many things about her. They were both physically attracted to each other, but there was more. He genuinely respected her. She was very intelligent and funny.

She liked the fact that he exhibited almost zero fear. He didn't seem afraid of a fight or of taking risks. He didn't even seem afraid of a nuclear meltdown, or if he was, he hid it well.

They made small talk and occasionally theorized about the situation that they found themselves in. As it began to lightly rain, they made their way back to the Forerunner. She fumbled in her purse for the keys. She found them and looked up at Bill. He brushed the rainwater from her face and then leaned in and kissed her.

Joe kept the fire low and stretched a tarp a few feet above the it and the firewood. He didn't know if it would work, be he didn't have much else to do. When he finished, he crawled inside the Jeep and took another drink from the canteen. Taylor and Beau also got in the Jeep, completely filling the small interior space of the vehicle.

Joe was worried about this young boy. His mom was here, but neither Joe nor his mom could protect him from the fallout of a nuclear materials release. Luckily, the boy was too young or just didn't care that this wasn't a campout but more of a camp for those who couldn't get out of town in time.

Joe tried to find a channel on the radio again, but he knew that it was useless. He wanted to entertain Taylor, or at least keep his mind off the situation. He considered giving the boy a survival manual, but it was getting dark. The only way to read would to be to use the dome light of the Jeep or flashlights. He didn't want to use any battery power that he didn't have to.

Joe was about to ask him what his favorite subject was in school or anything to get the kid to talk, when Taylor started the conversation. "My dog doesn't like the guy from the TV."

"What guy on TV?" Joe didn't understand what Taylor meant.

"The guy on TV who was here and was sitting under that tree all afternoon."

This set Joe out on a fit of laughter. He wondered if the vodka had helped this to be funny and decided that it hadn't. "Taylor, you have a very smart dog. Any dog that doesn't like politicians is at least as smart as many humans that I've met over the years." Joe went into another fit of laughter as he finished his sentence.

Hanna heard the laughing as she approached the Jeep. She knocked on the window. Taylor rolled it down. The old man had just finished a roll of laughter, which made her wonder what was in that canteen he was always drinking from. It didn't really matter to her. Joe had helped them so much in this nightmare, and he was good with Taylor and Beau.

"Time for bed," she told Taylor.

Taylor immediately protested, but Joe chimed in.

"Taylor, you need to do what your mom tells you to do."

Taylor immediately hopped out of the Jeep, and Beau followed.

Not wanting to have to argue with Taylor this evening, she quietly mouthed the word "thanks" to Joe. He smiled and winked in acknowledgement.

Hanna, Taylor, and Beau walked up the road and got in Cindy's car with her. As Hanna looked back at the campfire, it was going out. It seemed like an ominous sign of what their fate may hold in the next few days.

Carl Rothscoat's suit was getting damp from the rain. He didn't have a car here and was considering getting into a car with others to get out of the rain. The first car he approached had two women and a little boy inside.

As he got almost close enough to knock on the window, a large dog stood up and let out a bloodcurdling growl. Carl could see that the old dog was missing a few teeth but would not hesitate to take a chunk out of him if he opened the door. After seeing what the dog had done to his former carpool rider, Carl decided to move on.

He had walked in the rain for several more minutes when he found Tank passed out. The bandage on his knee was showing a splotchy red from where it had bled through. Carl knew better than to get into a car with him.

The rain and lack of alcohol had a clarifying effect on Carl. He no longer wished to kill anyone. He was worried more now than ever that someone may figure out that he killed his former political opponent, and he would be the number-one suspect.

He didn't believe that the sheriff or anyone else put much stock into his terrorist story. But it was the hand he had to play, and he would play it all the way to the lethal injection table if he had to.

He walked up to the next car, an old Chevy S-10. It had a Domino's sign on it. The occupant was nowhere to be found. There were other groups of people closer to the highway, he presumed. Maybe the driver of this truck had walked closer.

Carl tried the door, but it was locked. He considered smashing in one of the windows, but then the vehicle would be useless for keeping out the rain and would be cold.

He kept walking until he reached a Ford Bronco. The rear windows had a dark tint. The young man in the crucifix T-shirt was sitting at the wheel. A tattooed girl sat in the passenger seat. He thought they might offer him the chance to come out of the rain. Carl looked in the back of the truck to see the two young men whom he had taken the tray of doughnuts from.

"Four score and seven Bavarians ago, there was a doughnut shop full of maple-covered doughnuts." Dave started to lampoon the theft of the doughnuts in comparison to Lincoln.

The occupants of the car burst into laughter as Carl kept walking in the rain.

A few minutes later, a familiar vehicle was on his left. It was a Toyota Forerunner. The windows weren't tinted, but foggy. He remembered his teen years and decided he wouldn't be welcome in this car either.

He continued to walk for what seemed like ages. He came across other small camps of cars. They were almost all full of people. The ones who were awake looked at him warily. He kept walking.

In the distance, he could hear engines running and see the spotlights being used to search the area. He reached the end of the cars. The lights were attached to large camouflage generators that powered the lights pointing back toward the cars. Some of the soldiers were checking the generators and refueling them. It looked like many more soldiers were in tents. One with a rifle approached Rothscoat and asked him for ID.

"I'm the governor-elect!" Rothscoat blared.

The young soldier delivered him to the headquarters tent where he had a conversation with Captain Lofton and Sergeant Nash.

Captain Lofton spoke to him first. "I understand who you are, Mr. Rothscoat. But currently, the lieutenant governor is in charge and will be for several weeks until the election. Until then, you're a private citizen. You can stay here for the night and dry out, but in the morning, you need to go back to the citizens' area."

Carl's abger started to burn again. He was no longer cold, just wet. He wanted to attack Captain Lofton, but he knew it wouldn't help his situation. Plus, the sergeant who usually accompanied her looked like the type of guy that shouldn't be messed with.

Get it together, he thought. *You may not get to shake hands with army people on camera, but you are still going to be the governor. When that happens, you can make these people pay. It's time to dry out and regroup.*

CHAPTER 34

Geonwon was riding down the road in an eighteen-wheeler. Luckily, a truck driver who was in route to Atlanta had picked him up in Evansville. He introduced himself as Rob Hoopeston. Unfortunately for Geonwon, Rob had been in the U.S. Army and wanted to talk with him about all the recent changes in the army and Geonwon's thoughts about it. Geonwon kept changing the subject.

Luckily, the Americans didn't seem to be onto him yet. The news on the radio spoke of the siege at Red Hill but didn't list any suspects.

Geonwon told Rob that he was trying to get his citizenship by being in the army. Rob seemed pleased by this. He also noticed that Geonwon was constantly looking at his watch.

"We're still about six hours out from Atlanta," Rob told him,

Geonwon's constant watch-checking was a countdown to the time for the meltdown.

RED HILL

By now, the news was on every radio station.

"Isn't that some crazy shit?" Rob asked.

"Yes, it's insane." Geonwon didn't want to appear nervous. He told himself that there was no reason to be. The U.S. government had no idea who was hacking Red Hill, and he would be long gone before they figured it out.

CHAPTER 35

George Mendoza and Bob Felzer were running out of options and time. The United States Marine Corps had deployed CBIRF to the area, and the army had deployed the CST. These were the best that the U.S. had to offer in the event of a nuclear incident. The only problem was that these units were for when an event had already happened. George and Bob were trying to figure out how to stop the event from occurring.

"If we must use these guys, then we're already dead and have lost," Bob remarked out loud, but it didn't need to be said. He and George had been looking at code for the last several hours. They could locate the place in the code where they had lost control of the facility, but they could not regain it.

"Why did you stay?" George asked. "If we can't figure this out in another few hours, I'm out of here, and I suggest you do the same."

"I'm from here," Bob replied. "My father fought the Japanese in the Second World War. I was in the U.S. Navy. My children live here. We might lose this battle, but I will not give a single inch of this nation up to the enemy while I'm still breathing. You can leave any time you want, Mr. Mendoza, but I intend to spend my last breath, if needed, to shut down this reactor."

Mendoza had not witnessed that amount of patriotism since his time in the service. He didn't know if he felt as passionately as Bob did about the situation, but he was not about to give up.

CHAPTER 36

OCTOBER 31

The fire was all the way out. One by one, the people stranded outside of town woke up and walked to the firepit. Within an hour, Joe had it burning again.

"Does anyone know what tomorrow is and what will happen at noon?" asked Tank.

"You shut your mouth!" Joe screamed. He knew this might be the last day on Earth for the people stranded along the road, but he didn't want Taylor to see it coming. Joe was awake all night dreading the possibility of a slow death from radiation poisoning.

"Hold on, you old bastard. I'm not about to give a lecture. I was just going to say that considering the situation, we should have a party this evening." He looked over at Taylor and added, "A Halloween party. Some of us could run back to town and fetch some food and beer from the abandoned stores, candy too."

"Fine by me," Joe replied. His vodka stash was running low. He didn't know if he had enough to be completely blitzed when he died. Impending doom aside, he was not about to leave a shoddy-looking corpse. He had been a military man in his younger years, and old habits die hard.

He had heated another canteen cup of water. He took a razor and a can of Barbasol over to his Jeep and set it on the fender. He splashed the almost too hot water on his face and started to lather up.

Looking in the driver's-side mirror, he looked closely at his face. The coarse stubble had been gray for years. Once it was gone, he planned to comb his hair and find some more firewood. It would be a somber day for him. Gathering wood for the fire might keep his mind off it and maybe keep Taylor busy as well.

Ordinarily, Tim Baylor would have been the first to object, but considering the situation and the fact that the army had told him he no longer had arrest powers, he didn't. A cold beer or six might be the lubrication he needed to accept that he would not likely be alive past noon tomorrow.

The social norms and usual objections to a looting type of behavior had eroded over the last forty-eight hours. One of the last people anyone figured would have approved of looting was Janice Harmon. She said, "Bring me some various colored fabric, threads, and some scissors from the craft store, and I'll make Taylor a proper Halloween costume."

Frank Coleman responded. "I'll do just that." He hadn't considered going back into town to raid the businesses that he shopped at, but he figured that having the material would give

Janice something to do other than worry. It might also make a young boy's last night on Earth a little less sad.

Troy joined the excitement. "I say we do this, but we leave notes. That way, if they can stop the meltdown from happening, we can pay everyone back for what we took."

His sister Kara laughed. "Sure, Troy, whatever you say."

Shawn and Dave got into the Bronco with Troy and Kara. Yelena, Bill, and Tank got into the Forerunner, and the group headed back to town.

The first stop was the Texaco. Kara had locked it when she left. Surprisingly, no one had decided to loot it on the way out of town.

They fired up the pizza ovens. Troy grabbed all the Styrofoam coolers on the shelf and carried them across the street where Tank, Bill, and Yelena were offloading the contents of Rusty's Pub into the back of the Forerunner. There had to be at least forty cases of beer.

Tank went to grab some of the bottles of liquor from behind the bar when he spotted a shoe on the floor. He continued to walk around the bar. It was Rusty's foot. Rusty was staring at the ceiling in a permanent surprised gaze.

"Well, I guess we know what happened to Rusty," Tank joked.

"Don't be a dick. Of course, dying of natural causes might not be the worst way to go," Bill stated.

"Wow, since you got a little girlfriend, you sure have become a sensitive man."

"If we make it out of this alive, we can discuss the way I plan to live from now on. Until then, just take some booze and shut the fuck up," Bill said.

RED HILL

Tank laughed heartily as he stepped over the corpse of Rusty and grabbed the largest bottle of Jack Daniels he had ever seen. For good measure, he also grabbed a bottle of Maker's Mark.

The trio loaded the Forerunner with all the alcohol, ice, and coolers it could hold.

Troy and Kara were finishing up the pizzas and grabbing all the snack food from the Texaco. Troy stopped in the candy aisle. He grabbed all the Halloween candy that the store had. There was one kid in the group. This kid would get to celebrate Halloween tonight, and he was determined to make it a great one.

Shawn and Dave kept busy by following Frank Coleman. Frank threw a rock through the glass door of the craft store. They went inside and grabbed various fabrics and a sewing kit.

Within an hour, they were all finished. They all refueled their vehicles at the Texaco before they left, more out of habit than necessity.

Frank looked around the town. He could see that some of the people had decided to stay home. Not many, but some. He always questioned why some people would stay behind in a disaster when it meant imminent death. But then he shivered a little when he weighed that option against how much good it did to flee when they were blocked in.

Whether the meltdown occurred or not, the government was going to have a lot to answer for when this was over.

Only three stores appeared to have been looted in all the excitement of an evacuation. One was the craft store that Frank, Shawn, and Dave had just broken into. One of the others was Rusty's Pub, which was broken into by Tank, Bill, and Yelena. The third store was the local Waffle House. Considering that there is a Waffle House index that the government uses to determine how bad a disaster is, to see one abandoned and looted made Frank consider how dire their situation was.

Yelena walked up behind Bill and uncharacteristically said, "Waffles are terrible for you anyway."

Bill laughed and kissed her on the mouth.

The group climbed into their cars and headed back for the makeshift camp.

CHAPTER 37

Janice Harmon immediately started to sew when the group returned. It was one o'clock in the afternoon. As far as they knew, they all had about twenty-four hours before they would be forced to die a few miles from home while the U.S. government did next to nothing to help except keep them closer to the disaster.

Troy Felzer quietly tried to set up something he called "trunk or treat" for Taylor. He whispered his intentions to each of the vehicle owners, and they happily agreed. He spent the next few hours putting candy in the trunks of each car.

Joe, constantly seeking some sort of task to focus on, tried to restart the fire. It took him awhile, but he wasn't in a hurry. Taylor and Beau helped him with this.

He took another pull from his canteen. He wasn't surprised to see that the small law enforcement group had already started in on the supplies from the Forerunner. The group had been relatively quiet until now, but they were starting to make some noise. He wanted to tell them to slow down, but it would probably be their last night as well, and who was he to tell them to quiet down?

He was starting to get the fire going again. Taylor was starting to get bored.

"Do you remember how to find directions with a watch?" Joe asked Taylor.

"I do." Taylor then repeated the method and showed Joe which way was south.

"I'm now going to show you another way," Joe solemnly told him.

"But I can always use my watch," Taylor responded.

"What if it breaks or you lose it?" Joe asked.

"I don't know," Taylor replied.

"You'll need a straight stick and two rocks. It's called the shadow-tip method. But we're losing daylight, so we'll need to hurry, soldier," Joe instructed.

Taylor had never been called soldier. He liked it and set off to find two rocks and a straight stick.

CHAPTER 38

Tank's limp from the dog bite was gone. He was feeling very little pain. The large bottle of Jack Daniels was almost empty. He poured the rest of it on Joe's fire and opened the smaller bottle of Maker's Mark.

Taylor returned with a stick and two rocks. Joe took him to a relatively flat spot a few yards away to teach him the new land-navigation trick.

Troy was almost finished putting candy in cars, so Kara helped him with the last few cars. She was eating the last of a fun-size bag of Milky Ways when they walked back up to the group.

"That's a lot of chocolate," Dave teased her.

"Well, it's not like I have to worry about getting a big ass now," she jokingly replied.

"It looks pretty good from here," Dave said back.

They all started laughing.

RED HILL

Hanna had relaxed as well. She was eating a slice of pizza from the Texaco and drinking a beer from Rusty's Pub.

Janice had tried to ignore the increased drunkenness of the group. She had finished Taylor's Halloween costume. She didn't know what a Bash'em Badger was, and that was for the better. In the limited time, with the limited supplies she had available, she had made him a cowboy costume. She even made a fake saddle for Beau that doubled as a candy bag.

It was getting dark now. Taylor didn't quite understand the shadow-tip method yet. Joe took another pull from his canteen. With a tear in his eye, he promised Taylor he would show him again tomorrow. He hoped to hell someone could shut down the power plant, but if not, he would distract Taylor as long as he could.

Frank and Janice helped him put on his cowboy costume. Then they placed the candy bag saddle on Beau.

It was now 7:00 p.m.

Hanna fought back tears as she started walking with Taylor from trunk to trunk in search of candy. Many of the cars were abandoned. Other people were sitting around the fire, enjoying the supplies from the earlier trip back to town.

Troy went with her to make sure they found all the candy. He also made sure that he or Shawn was at each car so that Taylor could say "trick or treat" before getting candy.

The rest of the group was steadily demolishing the supplies from Rusty's Pub.

Dave and Kara were sitting together a few yards from the fire. Bill and Yelena were sitting on the other side sharing a bottle of Jim Beam.

Taylor and Beau, now finished trick or treating, were going through the Halloween treasure in their car, carefully supervised by Hanna. Left to his own devices, Beau would eat the whole stash. She knew that large amounts of chocolate could kill him, and she started weighing this in her mind. *You have to stop thinking like that,* she reminded herself. *It's not over yet.*

After looking around, she believed the rest of the group had decided it was over.

Tank was sprinting up small hills with no shirt on. He was yelling random sayings that were hard to understand.

Bill and Yelena must have decided to become an apocalypse couple. Dave and Kara must have done the same. Hanna hadn't seen Cindy or Shawn in a while, so she wondered if they might be having an end-of-the-world booty call as well.

Deputies Ford and Kepler were also not in attendance. She laughed out loud thinking about this.

Hanna took Taylor and Beau over to what she determined was the out-of-bounds area, which included Joe Reece, Frank Coleman, Janice Harmon, and Tim Baylor.

Frank and Tim were passing a bottle of Maker's Mark back and forth. Janice even took a small sip, shuddering as she swallowed, and then passed it back to Frank. He offered the bottle to Hanna. She promptly took a drink and almost didn't get it down.

As she offered the bottle to Joe, she said, "Joe, I want to thank you for being such a good friend to Taylor through all of this."

"Oh, no problem, but I will pass on the drink. I have my own." He took another hard swallow from the canteen.

RED HILL

Hanna laughed again. She had suspected the canteen was probably liquor, but now she knew.

As midnight became 1 a.m., some of the partygoers were still going strong, some were missing, and some were getting ready for bed.

It was now eleven hours until the meltdown was to take place.

CHAPTER 39

Back in Red Hill, very few lights were on, and only one car was on the road. It was a stolen Cadillac.

Roper Thompson hadn't possessed a driver's license in over ten years. But there was little risk of being caught tonight. He had watched the last of the law enforcement leave town the previous day.

This place was a looter's paradise. The smart money stuck with businesses. Those were all empty. No use getting shot trying to steal from a house when consumer goods, new in the box, were ripe for the taking. *Who cares if an alarm goes off? No one's going to respond.*

The Texaco was wide open. He was drinking a free slushy now as he drove around looking for expensive stuff to steal. He took a keg from Rusty's Pub. It was heavy.

Roper found another corpse. He smiled at his good fortune. Dead guys leaving him a lot of valuable stuff recently.

He stopped at Grover's Farm Supply. After throwing a trash can through the front window, he carefully entered the building. He had been permanently banned from Grover's due to his usual buying and stealing habits.

Roper was fond of the livestock syringes. This is where he went to today. *Happy Halloween! Clean syringes!* Stuffing his pockets with these and then some horehound candy, he carefully climbed back out through the window.

I wonder how much stuff I could fit in this car?

Roper put the Cadillac in reverse and backed through the front door. Two new MIG welders and some Yeti coolers fit into the trunk. Inside the coolers, he placed some of the more expensive tools, the ones he could pawn for the most cash.

After filling the back seat with similar items, the squatting Cadillac drove back to the park. *Time to enjoy one of these new syringes.*

As Roper was getting the chills, George Mendoza was now sweating. His tie was laying on the table in the control room. He walked outside. He could see the Marines and the army getting suited up, although he knew there was little that they could do. A mile or so beyond them, the fire department was likely preparing for the worst.

"I don't know what else we can do," George angrily said. "Maybe if we had ten more hours, we could get some sort of hotshot coder in here to fix this."

"Then go," Bob urged. "I'll try until it's over."

"Nah, I doubt I could get far enough away for it to make a difference now. I plan to keep working. Kind of like the band on the *Titanic*, don't you think?" George remarked.

"Maybe." Bob laughed.

CHAPTER 40

NOVEMBER 1, 7 A.M.

Roper Thompson knew some good places to lay low when he didn't have enough cash to stay at the Happy Hoosier. He figured it might be a good idea to hide the car and go to one of those places now. He hadn't been to them in a while.

He had used a place in an almost-abandoned strip mall on a regular basis. It used to be a Sears. Plus, it had private parking in back. He could stash the car and have a place to sleep.

Roper was feeling cold and sick. He approached the door. A new lock had been installed on the back door.

Roper dug around in the trunk until he found a tire iron. He used it to pry the latch. On the fifth try, the whole latch with the lock came off and landed on the ground.

The sound of a small engine was coming from inside of his hangout. *Should I go in? Surely, if someone is in here, they would have heard me pry off the lock. But it was locked from the outside.*

Roper stifled a cough when he entered the building. The blacked-out windows had one clean area at the bottom of the middle pane. He was less concerned with the window than all the stuff someone had left here. There were laptops. There were generators. The laptops weren't that great for pawning. But the eight generators in the room might as well be gold. Between the car, the stuff from Grover's, and the generators, he would get his fix and stay at the hotel for weeks.

Roper tried to pick up the first generator. It was still running, and he burned his hand. He didn't know where the off switch was. He didn't care. He had time. They could all run out of gas and cool off before he moved them. Besides, he was almost out of room in the Cadillac.

The laptops were new. He could tell by their appearance as well as the boxes they came in, which were still in the corner. There was a spot in the middle of the floor that was just urine and vomit.

Whose shit is this, and what is it doing here? If they don't come back soon, it's mine.

He swiped his finger across the mouse on the first computer. It was powered on and password-protected. The rest of them were as well.

He unplugged all of them. They continued to run on battery power. He moved all the computers to the passenger seat of the Cadillac. They were still close enough to the router to be connected to the internet.

He kept the doors closed to make sure that no one was watching him acquire his new merchandise. The noise of the eight generators was starting to annoy him and making his head hurt worse. He found their off switches. One by one, he turned off seven of the eight generators but left the eighth one on. This one powered the router that still connected the computers to the internet that was keeping Red Hill hostage. He didn't know this.

He found a light switch on the generator. *Nice. These are sweet generators. Surely, I can get a lot for them.*

Keeping the door closed, he sat down by the generator and considered what he should ask for them. Roper didn't know why he was so tired. The carbon monoxide helped the sound of the generator coax him off to sleep.

The computers still ran, although they were starting to lose power. Generator eight kept running; the three lights on the router were still green.

CHAPTER 41

Most of the people in the camp faced west. This is where they expected the mushroom cloud, or lack thereof, to be.

After awhile, they started giving up. Frank was rambling on about there being no mushroom cloud. Hanna, Taylor, and Beau were in their car. Dave had decided to ride his four-wheeler, which made Beau go crazy.

Tank had been passed out but then woke up and was ready to party again. This time, he started drinking beer. He proudly proclaimed that his favorite was the cold kind.

Bill walked out to the Forerunner with Yelena. He opened the driver's door, but Yelena couldn't see what he was doing near the console. Then he rolled down the windows, and the smooth sounds of the *Moody Blues Greatest Hits* crooned into the open. He laughed as he exited the vehicle.

"Don't laugh," Yelena scolded.

RED HILL

"I have this too," Bill replied as he grabbed her hands and gazed into her eyes.

"Unfortunately, he does," Tank yelled in the background.

The CD continued to play as Bill and Yelena danced slowly.

CHAPTER 42

Roper was dead and slumped over the small generator. The exhaust was burning his skin, making a putrid burning smell, but he didn't notice.

As gravity took over, his body pushed the generator on its side. It still ran. There was still enough gas in the tank to cover the suction tube that pulled the fuel from the tank to the engine.

By 10:00 a.m., most of the apocalypse couples had all disappeared again. The rest of the group sat around the fire.

"I hope my sons made it far away from here," Janice commented.

"I'm sure they did. They sound like smart guys. Are you cold?" Frank asked.

Janice nodded. Frank unzipped one of Joe's Polar sleeping bags and covered Janice up to her chin.

Joe was now making some instant hot chocolate in a canteen cup over the fire. Taylor had been gorging on his Halloween candy. Hanna would have normally rationed it out, but she didn't think it mattered at this point.

Joe was thinking the same thing, but he kept it to himself. He called Beau over and gave him the last of the beef jerky.

CHAPTER 43

Bob Felzer looked at the computer code again. George Mendoza was looking as well, but with less interest. He had decided that it was probably over.

"Who would do something like this? Who could?" Bob asked out loud.

"Many people would, but I don't know who could carry out this sophisticated attack." George looked up at the ceiling and then back to the computer screen.

"Russia might do something like this," George continued. "But we'll know if it was them by whether they go through with it or not. If it is the the Russians, then we'll live to see another day. They'll push us to the brink, but they haven't forgotten about mutually assured destruction. The whole Middle East would love to do something like this, but I don't know if they have anyone with this level of skill."

Bob gave him a bewildered look.

RED HILL

"It's hard to say. I had a theory about how it's being done, but I got shut down by the State Emergency Operations Center. They may have inadvertently aided the meltdown." George continued looking at computer code.

CHAPTER 44

The smell of burning flesh lingered in the empty Sears store as the small generator ran out of fuel. The router lights flickered a few times and then died. While the computers were still running in the trunk of the Cadillac, they were no longer connected to the internet.

Bob Felzer and George Mendoza regained control of the Red Hill Nuclear Power Plant reactor at 10:55 a.m. on November 1. They immediately enacted a SCRAM, which put the reactor in a safe configuration. They also regained control of the auxiliary systems surrounding the reactor. As soon as it was safe to do so, they powered down the equipment and physically locked it out.

Bob Felzer and George Mendoza had no idea why they regained control of the facility; they were just happy they did.

The CIBRF Marines, Army CST, and fire departments who had been dispatched to Red Hill had moved one mile back from the site. They were prepared to respond after the reactor overpressurized.

RED HILL

Bob Felzer had given the Marines the radio after notifying Incident Command to keep them informed of any changes at the plant.

George Mendoza was hungry. He started going through the lunchboxes of the control room operators who had evacuated the plant. He found the two things he wanted most in the world: a Mr. Goodbar and a pack of off-brand cigarettes.

The news that the reactor meltdown had been stopped didn't reach the camp until that afternoon. Everyone was looking at each other to determine if anyone was showing signs of radiation poisoning. At 5 p.m., the army turned off the frequency jamming technology. Several car radios came to life. Phones started beeping full of text messages and updates. Every radio channel was talking about the mysterious circumstances of the last few days and what would happen next. There were still no suspects.

Hanna hugged Taylor and Joe. Joe held back tears as he told Taylor that he knew everything would be fine.

Kara and Troy immediately called their father. He sounded like he had aged a few years in as many days. He told them that when he could turn over the plant, he was going to come home and rest, and then maybe take a small vacation with both of them.

Bill and Yelena were both feeling thankful. They had survived what could have been a grueling death and had oddly enough made a real connection. They loaded Tank up into her car, and after they made their way through the traffic, took him to a hospital in the next town.

Frank was suffering his first hangover in many years. He took Janice home and slept on her couch. He suffered nightmares about the event for several months.

Deputy Ford, who despised camping, just wanted a shower. She piled into the police car with Tim Baylor and Deputy Kepler to head back to town. As they were about to drive away, Tim Baylor spotted Shawn. He rolled down his window and yelled, "Hey, do you know where we could get some decent doughnuts?"

"I think so," Shawn replied with a grin. There was apt to be a lot of law enforcement in town, and they were not going to miss this opportunity.

EPILOGUE

Captain Lofton was given the order for her and her soldiers to return to base for a debriefing. They removed the roadblock from the interstate. The FBI was called in to investigate the deaths of Private Jason Hong and Governor Irwin Poole.

The death of Private Hong was never proven to be directly connected to the occurrences at Red Hill, but the FBI had some theories that they were not able to conclusively prove. The murder of Governor Poole remained a mystery that was never solved. People speculated, as people do in small towns, and sometimes large towns.

Rusty of Rusty's Pub fame had succumbed to a heart attack. Roper Thompson was posthumously awarded the Red Hill Citizen of the Year Award. This made Tim Baylor upset. Tim had arrested him for theft, drugs, and fighting several times. But the town council reminded him that without Roper, Red Hill might be a smoldering wasteland. In the end, Tim had no choice in the matter.

RED HILL

Roper had no living relatives left in the area, so the town chipped in for the funeral and had the award encased beside his tomb at the cemetery. The local pastor noted in the ceremony that, for all the things that Roper had taken, he had returned to them so much more.

Hanna and Taylor moved from Red Hill to Indianapolis when her job was downsized. They keep in contact online with most of the people they were stranded with in those frightening days in the fall of 2016.

Joe Reece lost Bull Creek Military Supply in 2017. He was glad to be rid of it. He placed the closed sign in the window one final time, got in his Jeep, and went home to enjoy a simple retirement. He would send Taylor a card every year for Taylor's birthday for the rest of his years.

Janice Harmon passed in the spring of 2019. It was a simple funeral. In her will, she made several requests. Pimento cheese sandwiches and coconut cake had to be served at her wake. The will didn't specify why. Her sons believed it was the early signs of dementia. But these were Frank's favorite foods that Janice would often make for him. The sandwiches and cake made by the caterers tasted different to Frank, adding to the sense of sadness at losing his friend. Change is constant, he mused, but some changes are much harder than others.

Janice's last will and testament included the provision that her estate be divided into thirds. One third of the money went to Frank Coleman, who had changed his mind about travelling and decided to go camping in the Rocky Mountains. The money that she left him helped him buy an Airstream, which he affectionately named Janice.

Tank Porter got into a fight with another patron when Rusty's Pub reopened. Tank beat the man badly enough that his lawyer told him he couldn't claim self-defense. He'll be eligible for parole in 2021.

Bill Reilly and now Yelena Harris Reilly visit Tank on occasion. They're expecting their first child in a few more months. Bill stopped selling guns and became an electrician.

Troy Felzer joined the navy after all. When he finished seminary school, he became a navy chaplain. His dad and sister couldn't be prouder.

Kara Felzer and Shawn Graves decided that they had just been an apocalypse couple. Kara became friends with Yelena Harris, who talked her into going to school to become a nurse.

Cindy Peller became a flight attendant. She had always liked to travel, and the events surrounding Red Hill reminded her that life is a gift to be cherished and not hurried through.

Deputies Anna Ford and Jerry Kepler agreed to never speak to each other about their meltdown fling again. It was awkward for them to work together after that. Anna stayed at Red Hill Police Department. Jerry Kepler became an EMT and joined the fire department.

5 to 2 Doughnuts never became a franchise, but it did eventually make enough money to add a second store. Shawn and Dave didn't become millionaires, but they lived comfortable lives in Red Hill.

Bob Felzer retired from Red Hill Nuclear Power Plant. He then wrote a book about the incident that gripped the nation in fear and forever altered conversations about the safety of nuclear power.

Tim Baylor lost reelection for sheriff. He became a realtor while working as a part-time officer.

George Mendoza was right. He was never promoted above his current job. In 2018, he left the Nuclear Regulatory Commission to teach college. He doesn't miss working for the NRC.

The Miami Herald, November 3, 2016, Page A8

A young man was found dead from a single gunshot wound to the head in the Hilton Hotel on Biscayne Boulevard this morning. He was wearing a U.S. Army uniform, possibly bought at a secondhand store. The U.S. Army has declared that the deceased is not and hasn't at any time been in the U.S. Army. Police said that they will release new information when it becomes available.

The Indianapolis Independent Press, June 23, 2018, Page A1

The police were called to the Governor's Mansion yesterday when one of the housekeepers placed a call to 911. When the police arrived at the scene, 19-year-old Andrea Pine was found brutally murdered. Andrea was a political science major at Indiana University and an intern for Governor Rothscoat. The police have listed him as a suspect.

BENSON JACKSON

The Indianapolis Independent Press, November 19, 2018, Page A1

Governor Rothscoat is expected to resign as governor on Tuesday. He is being tried for first degree murder in the death of Andrea Pine, a former intern for the governor. Rumors of an affair between Governor Rothscoat and Miss Pine had been circulating around the Governor's Mansion for some time when the incident occurred. Governor Rothscoat was a suspect in the death of his predecessor, Governor Irwin Poole, but he was never charged for the crime.

ABOUT THE AUTHOR

Benson Jackson is an emergency preparedness professional. Former military, he has worked in the field of destroying chemical weapons for close to twenty years. He has two undergraduate degrees in emergency preparedness and homeland defense and a master's degree in occupational safety from Eastern Kentucky University. Ben lives in Kentucky where he enjoys home remodeling projects and spending time with his wife Jennifer and their three dogs.

Bensonjackson.com
bensonjacksonauthor@gmail.com
Bluedoorpublishing.co

Made in the USA
Monee, IL
04 May 2021